SINKIRA

A Masai Outcast Reclaimed

Gail Walker

Pacific Press Publishing Association
Mountain View, California
Oshawa, Ontario

Cover design and illustration: Ed Guthero

Printed in United States of America

Library of Congress Cataloging in Publication Data

Walker, Gail
Sinkira.

1. Munke, Daniel. 2. Converts, Seventh-day Adventist—Kenya—Biography. I. Title.
BX6189.M86W34 1984 248.2'46'0924 [B] 83-23639
ISBN 0-8163-0552-8

Dedicated

to my son Leonard and his wife, Betty, who introduced us to Pastor Sinkira and his family, and who assisted by checking the manuscript for errors, and to my husband, Irwin, for his tireless assistance.

Contents

Sinkira wearing the traditional dress of a Masai warrior.

His Name Shall Be Sinkira

The small Masai village in southwest Kenya buzzed like a hive of bees. Warriors readied their spears, women cooked *ugali,* a thick porridge made of ground maize, while ox meat simmered over open fires.

Blood, drawn the day before from the cattle and mixed with milk and a little brown sugar, had clotted firm enough to be sliced like bread. The women prepared it to serve to the warriors. The *laibon,* or witch doctor, guaranteed it would give them added strength, and each wife and mother wanted her warrior to have much strength and the goodwill of the gods with him as he went out from the village.

Everything had been made ready for the evening festivities. Nentayia, the wife of Napangala, stood in the doorway of her hut watching the other villagers scurrying about. She well knew that a war party would soon be going out—quite likely that very night. She also knew that the sense of foreboding she felt at times like these almost overwhelmed her. This time her sense of foreboding seemed even greater. She dared not speak a word of this to her husband, the father of her five-year-old daughter, Nemitil, and also of the little girl who had died at the age of one year, but more important, the father of the child soon to be born—she hoped, the man-child Munke Napangala dreamed of day and night. The man-child would carry on the family name.

Napangala, one of the wealthiest men in the village, owned many cattle, sheep, and goats. The people often sought his advice in time of trouble. The tribe revered Napangala and respected him for his wisdom, strength, and prowess, both when hunting and when in battle.

Nentayia tried to press her fears back to the recesses of her mind as she joined the group of women preparing this important feast to be eaten before their warriors went to raid a neighboring Kisii village.

Surely, Nentayia thought, there should be an end of this feuding. Only last month the Kisii had raided their village, killing a warrior and wounding others. Now her husband would lead the Masai in a battle of revenge. When would it all end?

Soon the warriors hurried to the stream. Nentayia heard them laughing and talking of their bravery as they decorated their bodies with clay in readiness for the battle. This was their custom.

When the warriors returned, the women served them their meal. Repeatedly they went to the container filled with *pombe,* a strong alcoholic beverage. Soon most of them began talking too loudly, and their laughter became raucous. They bragged among themselves about what they would accomplish at the Kisii village.

As Nentayia walked among them serving meat, milk, *ugali,* and blood pudding, she felt her child stir within her, and her uneasiness returned. Why couldn't she rid herself of this sense of foreboding?

As darkness fell, the warriors began their war dance, and with one final shout, grabbed their *orinkas* or clubs, and spears, and disappeared into the night.

The women put away the remaining food and quietly made their way to the family huts, where their children would be sprawled on the floors, sleeping in total oblivion of the activities of their elders. The mothers stumbled over the sleeping children and shoved them to the side, as they felt their way to their beds, there to await the return of their warriors.

Nentayia found Nemitil asleep in her usual place. She lay down with a sigh on her crude bed. But no amount of turning helped her find a comfortable way to lie. Finally, she dozed off and dreamed wild, terrifying dreams until she heard the men returning after midnight with jubilant shouts and loud talking.

She listened as they talked of taking the Kisii by surprise. They had killed one man, and that redeemed the Masai killed by the Kisii. Soon the village became quiet again, as, one by one, the men entered their huts and dropped into a sleep of exhaustion.

As Napangala entered their hut, he answered Nentayia's unasked question, "We all returned, with no man killed."

Nentayia wondered where it would end. These border skirmishes and night raids had been going on longer than her people could remember. But a flood of relief came to her with the realization that her Napangala had returned safely. Sleep came at last.

In the morning the warriors, although still elated, were sobered somewhat after their night raid, the *pombe* having worn off. But they had no idea that the Kisii had tracked them to their village. Suddenly at the first cry of battle, the formerly brave Masai fled like cowardly hyenas.

However, Napangala, concerned for his wife with child and his little daughter, stayed behind in an attempt to defend them from the Kisii warriors. He fought bravely, savagely, but when the Kisii retreated, his mother found his body where it had fallen, pierced by many spears.

At once she began the death wail, and soon the other village women joined her, all wailing, screaming, and crying. Children joined the mournful din, and the warriors, knowing the Kisii had fled, crept back to the village, fearful of what they would find.

When Nentayia knelt beside her dead husband's body, again her child moved restlessly within her, and her heartbreak became even more intense. This child, as yet unborn, would never have a father. Even if it were the man-child both Napangala and she had wanted, he could never inherit any of his father's wealth, because his father had died before his birth.

Nentayia, who had been one of the leaders among the village women, would now be a nobody. She would have nothing but her bridal gifts, the nine cattle given her by Napangala, and their offspring. She would have nothing more. At the present this concerned her little. She had just lost her husband. Grief overwhelmed her.

Immediately the other warriors began doing the necessary and ritualistic duties. Some went for material to form a crude box for Napangala's body. Others began digging a grave in an appropriate place, while others, including some of the women, prepared his body for burial.

They took off all of the ornaments worn around his neck and wrists. These indicated his bravery through the many rituals of his life, and Nentayia's heart broke when she saw them removed.

They shaved Napangala's head and smeared it with fat taken from an ox slaughtered for this purpose. Then they wrapped his body-sheet about him and placed him in the rough coffin, closing the lid forever.

Several warriors moved the coffin to the burial grounds, with the entire village following, continuing the death wail, which grew louder and more intense as they lowered the coffin into the open grave.

Some of the men went into the forest where they found a tree named the *oloigero* tree. They stripped some of its leaves from its branches and upon returning scattered these leaves on top of the coffin. This completed the death ritual. Now they covered the coffin with earth.

From that time onward, no member of Napangala's family dared use any part of the *oloigero* tree. His family now considered this tree sacred to them, and its use would bring a curse upon the member who broke the custom.

The feast prepared for such occasions began following the burial, and for four days the entire village mourned the loss of their brave leader. Wailing continued throughout the days and nights, as the women cooked much meat, *ugali,* and a few vegetables. The women at first comforted Nentayia, then left her alone.

The warriors drank much *pombe* along with the prepared food. Returning to the *pombe,* they drank themselves almost insensible. Losing Napangala had hurt them all deeply. They had respected him, not only as a warrior, but as a mighty man in the village. They must mourn him appropriately because of his stature among the villagers.

The elders took the ornaments that meant so much to Nentayia and gave them to different relatives. Nothing did she or her daughter, Nemitil, get of Napangala's ornaments. Nentayia understood the custom, but it reminded her that from now on her life would be changed completely.

Alone she entered her hut to find Nemitil crying as if her heart would break. "My child, such is the custom of our people." Nentayia's gentle voice gave little comfort to her daughter, too young to understand that women and girls inherit nothing and are chattel upon the death of a husband and father. After four days the mourning ended; the villagers returned to their routines. But Nentayia's grief lasted much longer.

The new life within her became heavier each day. She knew that soon her time would come, and she attempted to get extra rest. But in the village the people, her husband's people, were quarreling over her dead husband's vast herd of cattle. Each wanted a portion, and with no close relatives to claim it as his rightful inheritance, the elders distributed the herd among the villagers.

Nentayia attempted to be there each time someone took an animal, and when she saw them eyeing her cows, she fought to save them. They belonged to her, not to Napangala, and she managed to rescue most of them.

"Those cows give me great comfort," she confided to Nemitil. "Your father, on the day of our marriage, gave them to me, and they bring me happiness and food." She sighed as she remembered.

Now that she had no one to take care of her, her daughter, or her coming child, the cows not only reminded her of the love of Napangala, but they remained between herself and starvation.

Nemitil helped her gather firewood to cook the little remaining maize. Nentayia gathered wild vegetables, but as she became heavier and more awkward, these tasks became more difficult.

The village people began asking, "What do you plan to do, now that you no longer have a wealthy husband to support and care for you? You know it is the custom of the Masai that you should return to your own village."

"I intend to remain here and raise my family in the village of my husband," she replied.

"But this is not the custom of our fathers," one of the villagers protested.

"You must return to your own village, the village of your fathers," Napangala's mother insisted.

When Nentayia refused to leave, her mother-in-law began to whisper to the other villagers, "Nentayia has small wisdom. We'll see how long she stays when we get through with her!" She sneered as she talked to others.

The villagers forced Nentayia to walk farther for her water or to wait until last to fill her gourd, and in other ways made life miserable for her. When her supply of maize ended, she attempted to barter for more. "No maize for anyone who brings us small joy," one spoke, and others agreed. One or two offered her maize, but their barter price was much too high.

To Nentayia's dismay her mother-in-law began taking Nemitil to her hut, sometimes to stay overnight, and each time, when the child returned, Nentayia could sense the child's attitude toward her slowly changing, causing cold fingers of fear to creep into her heart.

One day while milking, Nentayia realized her time had come. Finishing her milking, she returned to her hut to lie down and rest. "Nemitil, you give me great joy in being here. Go, bring the midwife," she said, trying to keep calm. Then she lay back to wait.

Pain after pain gripped her, leaving her drained and still waiting for the return of her daughter. Fear pressed against her as she rested between pains, which were becoming closer and more urgent. Would a midwife come to her aid, or would she have to bear this child alone, as she had been alone since the death of her husband?

Finally Nemitil entered, followed by an older woman. Help at last! Nentayia recognized the woman as the same midwife who had attended her when she bore her girls. She thought of the birth of the two girls. How differently the village people had treated her then!

Another stronger contraction brought Nentayia back to the present, and she gripped the side of her bed. She dared not utter a sound, as the midwife would consider it a sign of weakness. Even in childbirth, a woman must be brave.

The midwife could see that Nentayia's time drew near, and she ushered Nemitil and a few curious villagers out of the hut. As the contractions became stronger and closer together, Nentayia found it more difficult to lie still. But each time she turned in the bed the midwife shouted, "Lie still!" and she beat her with a special stick brought for that purpose.

Nentayia wanted to scream out, but she knew that to do so would endanger her own life as well as that of her unborn child, so she suffered patiently and silently. She hid her relief when at last a lusty cry brought several villagers rushing back into the hut.

A successful delivery! The gods were smiling upon Nentayia today. The villagers congratulated the midwife, and relief flooded over Nentayia as she cuddled her baby, a man-child, in her arms.

"I will keep him from unhappiness. He is comfort to my aching heart," she told herself.

The midwife, having completed her duties, stepped outside to announce, "Nentayia has just delivered a man-child." With that, she returned to her hut.

Nentayia lay there wondering, "What will the villagers do now? This is not a day of joy for them. My son must have a name, but will the women allow him the right to a respectable name?"

Often children born following one that has died were given the name of the cowardly hyena, *olkonoi,* and she knew of many children bearing that unpleasant name. She knew that the village mothers as they returned to their huts would consider *Olkonoi* a fit name.

Nentayia heard some of the talk. "If she had only returned to her home village, we wouldn't have to be choosing a name," said one. Another disagreed, saying, "Remember, Napangala's first man-child could possibly become a mighty warrior like his father. We mustn't forget that."

Finally a leader among the women spoke: "The *manyatta* [young men's training village] is about to be dismissed. Let us give this man-child a worthy name." The other women nodded their heads and grunted in agreement.

One older woman went for some milk, a part of most Masai ceremonies, and they hurried to the hut of Nentayia, where they went through the birth and name ceremony. When they nicked the baby's ear, indicating that he followed a dead child, Nentayia's heart nearly turned to ice. The women would most certainly give him a cowardly name.

After the rituals and ceremony concluded, one of the women solemnly announced, "His name shall be Sinkira."

Sinkira! It pleased Nentayia, and she thanked them saying, "The name is good. It gives me great joy."

But the women were already moving out of the hut, leaving her alone with her newborn son. Sinkira! That showed great respect. She felt much gratitude that the village women had chosen such a name. Realizing that the *manyatta* would soon be dismissing, she felt fortunate indeed that her little boy chose to arrive at that time.

Nentayia moved to a more comfortable position, pulled the warm animal skin closely about her son and herself, and dropped into a sleep of oblivion.

Hours later she wakened to Sinkira's crying. Startled at first, she soon remembered the happenings earlier in the day and rose to take up her regular duties. There would be no one to cut wood for her fire, milk her cows, or gather a few wild vegetables for her to eat. All help had stopped with the death of her husband, and Nentayia lived in constant dread. The birth of this child would not change things. What would be the future of this little one, so badly wanted before Napangala's death by both of them? What more would her mother-in-law do to attempt to force her to return to her former village alone? Should she have left Nemitil and gone before this man-child had come? But if she had done so, Napangala's name would have died forever, and she couldn't bear that thought.

Nentayia knew only one thing—she would be the best possible mother for Sinkira. Her motherly intuition told her that one day he would distinguish himself in some way. Had she fully realized the sacrifice she would have to make to keep her son, she would have done no differently. She vowed that she would see that Sinkira became everything Napangala would have wanted of his son. She could do no more than that.

An Unbearable Existence

Nentayia moved about as one in a trance. There was little food in her hut. Her own daughter, Nemitil, spent more and more time with the grandmother, and when she did come home for short visits she showed less and less respect for her mother. Nentayia, shunned by her former friends, harrassed by her mother-in-law, and still grieving for her beloved husband, felt she had little to live for—but there was Sinkira, her newborn man-child!

Nentayia's cows produced less and less milk, and this caused her great worry. However, her mother-in-law, in spite of her apparent hostility, must have felt some obligation to her dead son's wife, for every few days either she herself or Nemitil would take a little milk to Nentayia—enough for one day—and with the small amount of milk they brought would say, "This is all you will get for two or three days."

One by one men went to her hut offering to marry her, but Nentayia refused. She could become a second or third wife. "I appreciate your offer, but if I marry you, Munke Napangala's name will forever be gone, as would his father's before him," she always answered.

She knew that Napangala and little Sinkira were the only sons in the family, and should she do anything to change her son's position, the family name, Munke, would die out completely, so Nentayia held fast to her decision.

Her mother-in-law continually tried to force her to return

to the village of her childhood. But Nentayia, knowing that her children must remain in the village of their father, refused to leave. Such was the way of their forefathers, and she could not bring herself to leave Sinkira with the grandmother. The child brought great comfort to her.

One day when the mother-in-law took them a bit of milk, Nentayia timidly asked, "Could we have a bit of maize also?"

At this the mother-in-law flew into a rage, ranting, "You are no joy to me." And she beat her unmercifully. "Go home!" she shouted as she rushed out of the hut.

Nentayia lay unconscious upon the floor of the hut for several hours. Sinkira wakened and began to cry. But no one went to their aid. When Nentayia regained consciousness and nursed him again, she realized that her life could be in real danger. Yet she determined, knowing it was against Masai custom, to remain in the village to be with her son.

At the stream one day, she overheard some of the village women gossiping. "Did you know that Nentayia will soon return to her village?"

"Yes, another woman will bear children as heirs for Napangala."

"How can this be?" another asked.

"One of his cousins will father the children, and according to our custom, Napangala's name can continue. His mother has spoken."

Nentayia hurried back to her hut without the water. Worry made tight knots in her stomach. Could this really be true?

Then she heard that the village elders had told her mother-in-law, "Because Nentayia has already borne Nemitil before Napangala's death, and later, Sinkira, his own son, your plan is not a plan of wisdom. It is contrary to Masai custom."

Had Nemitil or Sinkira not been living, her mother-in-law

could have accomplished her desires. However, Nentayia knew this would not discourage the women. Her mother-in-law refused to give up and swayed a lot of the village people to her idea that Nentayia should be made to return to the village of her fathers. Now the persecution intensified.

It seemed that Nentayia's stomach never felt pleasure, and Sinkira nursed almost constantly—always hungry. Much time had passed since Nentayia had anything to barter. In spite of her hatred, the mother-in-law sent small amounts of milk to the hut, but threats always accompanied the milk. "Nentayia, you must leave, or worse will happen." Each time Nentayia refused, she would be severely beaten.

Sinkira toddled about now, but each time anyone entered the hut, he cowered in the corner. He knew that terrible things happened to his mother. As he grew older he tried to defend her. When the sticks were turned upon him, he again retired to his corner, hoping no one would notice him.

How Nentayia wished that Napangala had at least one brother! All of Napangala's wealth would have gone to him, and he would have taken care of them, as a good Masai. But wishing didn't change anything. More and more men continued asking her to marry them.

Nentayia, still a lovely young woman, could have taken the easy way out, but she continued to decline. She had been the only wife of Napangala, and she had no desire to become a second or third wife of another man.

"Why are you so stupid?" the village people asked. "You have no wisdom in your head," and again, they beat her unmercifully.

Many days passed before she could leave her bed, and little Sinkira cared for her alone. He gathered a few little sticks to make a fire, and he had learned where to find some of the wild plants they ate. With these, and the little milk the mother-in-law still took to them, he nursed his mother back to partial health.

"My mother, eat to become strong again," he coaxed.

"I no longer care to live," Nentayia whispered.

"But, my mother, what will become of me if you die?" Sinkira asked.

"Just for you, my son, just for you. For myself, I no longer care to live." And Nentayia ate small portions for the sake of Sinkira.

Due to malnutrition and the abuse at the hands of the villagers, Nentayia never completely recovered enough to care for things as she once had, and her cows no longer gave milk.

The time came when the child feared to leave his mother to go for sticks and wild plants, because she had become so weak and helpless she could do nothing for herself. He also feared what the villagers might do.

One day Konoi, an older relative, went to their hut and stated, "Sinkira, from now on you must herd cattle each day."

Nentayia still owned a few of her herd, so Sinkira, although younger than most of the herd boys, included his mother's cattle with the others given him for attention and spent the entire day grazing them. As he followed the cattle, he looked for a plant they called *inderema*. This he picked and took home to boil for an evening meal after work.

Many days Sinkira went to herd cattle on an empty stomach, leaving Nentayia also hungry, and neither of them ate until he took the *inderema* home at night. There were nights when he came home empty-handed, but in spite of these trials, Nentayia continued living in the village, and Sinkira now determined that his mother remain where he could care for her.

Nentayia developed a crippling disease. Unable to leave her bed, the burden of everyday living fell upon Sinkira's young shoulders. One evening he spoke of something on his heart: "My mother, I have heard it said that in a hospital you could get some comfort."

"And I have also heard, my son. But we have no money, nor could I walk so far. There is no one to help us."

"But, my mother, how far is it?" Perhaps I could carry you."

"The closest hospital I know of is at Narok, and it is very far. It is at least one hundred miles. You could never carry me that far, my son."

"Yes, my mother, I also see there is no way," responded Sinkira.

Since the Masai owned many cattle, the grass near the village became more sparse, so the herd boys took them farther and farther away from home. They searched for places where grass grew more abundantly. Each took his herd in a different direction and spent the day alone.

It took longer to reach the grass at this time of the year, and often Sinkira would be gone all day. Nentayia, crippled and ill, waited for his return each evening. Sometimes he would find some *ilamuriak,* a seasonal fruit they enjoyed. He picked all he could carry and turning his body-sheet up by the corners, filled it with the delicious fruit.

The days he found this fruit they ate well in the evening, but it was in season only a short time, and again famine haunted them.

One evening Sinkira hurried home in great excitement. Among his finds of the day was his mother's favorite kind of mushroom. "My mother, see what I brought for you!" he exclaimed. But she did not respond. Nentayia lay motionless on the bed.

Sinkira shook her, but again there was no sign of life, and his first thought was, "My mother is dead. What can I do to bring her back to life again? My mother is the only one who loves me. What will I do if she is dead?"

He shouted to her and shook her again, but her body remained limp. Remembering her hunger that morning, he cut a small piece of the mushroom and placed a bit of it in her mouth. It remained where he put it, on her tongue. Now, thoroughly frightened, he started screaming and crying for help until at last some of the villagers went to see why Sinkira bothered them with his crying. He explained, "I have been out herding all day, and when I came home I found my mother like this. Is she dead? Can any of you help me bring her to life?"

Sinkira, unaccustomed to asking for help or receiving any, begged in desperation, and a woman left the little hut, returning in a short time with a little milk. Opening Nentayia's mouth, she poured a little in, drop by drop. As it trickled down her throat, Nentayia regained consciousness and finally spoke to Sinkira. "My son, stop crying. I only fainted."

When she spoke, villagers left the hut, obviously disgusted. Sinkira cooked the mushrooms and fed his mother, bit by bit, but she remained very weak. Later that evening, after everyone in the village had retired, Sinkira sneaked over to the place where the villagers made the *pombe*, scooped up the discarded dregs, and returned home.

Building a small fire, Sinkira put these dregs into some water and boiled them. This he fed to Nentayia, and gradually she felt new life flowing into her body.

Although Nentayia could do little to help Sinkira, she taught him to be honest, obedient, and respectful to the elders, especially the *laibon,* or witch doctor. "The *laibon* is like a god to us Masai," she declared. "He can predict things to come and help you when you are ill. Never forget that he can also do terrible things to one who annoys him. Never, never annoy a *laibon*. However, remember that when someone is sick, he can also help them get well again."

Remembering this, one time when Nentayia's joints were especially swollen and painful, Sinkira called the *laibon* and asked if he would go and help his mother. The *laibon* knew their situation well, but agreed to go to the little hut anyway.

He entered the hut and placed in the center of the room the leather-seated stool he carried. Then he poured a little milk onto the seat. From his pocket he drew out some small sticks, placed them in the milk, and began calling on all the ancestors to help this sick woman.

Sinkira remembered, as he heard the names being called, that Nentayia often called upon these same ancestors when she needed special help—either relief from her pain or lack of food—and he realized that both the *laibon* and his mother believed that in some way these ancestors could help them. He couldn't understand how a dead person could come back and help someone sick or in trouble. His father was dead; why didn't he come back to help them?

When the *laibon,* who knew of their pitifully poor situation, demanded one of Nentayia's few remaining cows in payment for his services, Sinkira wished he had never called the man. His incantations did Nentayia no good, and she remained bedfast and in constant pain.

Sinkira tried to put all the pieces together, like a puzzle. All his people believed in gods. Some of his friends were beginning to attend school, schools operated by the African Inland Mission but partially funded by the Kenya government. Kipkirir, one of his friends, told him one day, "They tell us in school about a loving Father in heaven who cares about everybody, even little boys who must work very hard."

Sinkira wondered, "If there is such a Father, why does He allow the *laibon* to place curses on people who annoy him or on a person someone pays him to curse?"

"I do not know that answer," Kipkirir responded, "but I shall try to learn." Each day Kipkirir told Sinkira more of what he had learned about the Father in heaven.

The number of cattle in Sinkira's herd increased as more of the boys began attending school. Sometimes he ran all day long, trying to keep the herd together. One day, after grazing the cattle some distance from the river, he drove them back for a drink. After they drank their fill, he started driving them back to graze. As the cattle followed the winding trail among the thorny bushes to the grassy meadow beyond, he constantly watched for wild animals that could endanger either the herd or himself. The bushes touched above the path, making it quite dark, and he had driven the cattle about halfway when he saw a huge tusk coming out of the bushes just a few yards ahead of him.

He turned and bolted thinking, "That is a big animal. If I cannot run faster than it can, I am in deep trouble. It must be a rogue elephant."

The elephant started after Sinkira. The boy heard it crashing through the undergrowth as he ran for his life. He continued running! Thorns tore at his clothing, his arms, and his legs. He tired and then heard a voice behind him shout, "You can run faster than the elephant. Keep on running."

He didn't dare look back to see who had spoken to him, but sped even more rapidly. When he neared the village, the elephant gave up and turned back.

Sinkira told Nentayia, "A voice spoke to me telling me to run very fast. Do you think that was the voice of Kipkirir's God?"

His mother simply shook her head. She couldn't answer him. She knew even less than he about this God, but she rejoiced that Sinkira remained alive and with her.

Although still terrified, Sinkira had to go in search of the cattle. The elephant had disappeared, and at last he found the cattle grazing peacefully. He stayed until almost sundown before driving them home. For days he was puzzled about the voice that had spoken to him. No one in the village knew anything about it.

All Masai boys and girls between five and eight years of age go through a ritual called "cutting of the teeth." This is the first of several rituals Masai children endure before the time of the really big one of their lives, the circumcision.

Before that they must show their bravery in other ways.

The elders decided when the time came for the removal of the two lower teeth. It didn't matter that the teeth would have come out by themselves in a couple years' time. It was most important that this cutting be done before they lost their first tooth, so custom dictated.

If the children could endure this pain and show bravery, their relatives gave them many gifts of goats, sheep, and even cows. For the first time the children could own something of value, so it was of utmost importance to them and their parents that the children show their bravery.

The elders set the day and took the children to the village center. One by one they were taken to an elder who with a knife cut out two of the front teeth in the lower jaw. The children were given nothing for pain; yet if one cried out, he would receive no gifts. It disgraced not only the child but also the entire family, should the child show any sign of fear.

Sinkira belonged to the age group of the children, who were to have their teeth cut out. He reluctantly went with the others. As he watched the elder cutting the teeth with his knife, he saw blood running down the chins of his friends and thought, "This is terrible!"

Some stepped forward bravely, others were dragged and firmly held. When it came Sinkira's time he said, "No, I don't agree to have my teeth removed."

An elder attempted to drag him, but he held back, crying and fighting the elders. At five, Sinkira didn't stand a chance. When it was all over, the brave children received their gifts, but Sinkira received nothing but contempt.

In spite of the pain from having his front teeth cut out, he took the cattle out the next day and the days following. Now in addition to his mother's going against tribal custom, her son, Sinkira, had attempted to break with custom, and the village boys made fun of him, the elders considered him a coward, and times became more difficult than ever.

When he came in from herding one evening, his grandmother saw him carrying a stick he had broken from the *oloigero* tree to help him guide the cattle. She began to weep. "Who told you to use this stick? This is a forbidden stick for us. It will bring a curse upon you. Leaves from this tree were used in your father's grave."

"No one told me not to use it," Sinkira answered, as he threw it far away, but his grandmother continued, "That *oloigero* tree will get you in trouble for sure!"

Sinkira worried about this curse for several days, wondering what terrible things would happen to him. However, after some time passed and nothing happened, he forgot his worry. But he never forgot that that tree was forbidden to him and his family.

During the rainy season the numbers of mosquitoes increased, and many people became ill with malaria. One day Sinkira went home very ill. His head ached. His stomach hurt. He ran a high fever, but no one cared for him or gave him any help. The hospital was far away, too far away to take a nobody. Nentayia worried but could do nothing but cry for help. However, the villagers all ignored her.

Sinkira grew weaker and suffered a great deal, and one day as Nentayia cried for help, an old man passing through the village heard her and went to see if he could do anything to help. He prepared a bitter juice and tried to get Sinkira to drink it. At the first taste he recoiled, but he lacked the strength to resist. At times he became delirious, but the stranger continued making more juice of the *entulelé* berries, forcing Sinkira to drink it a little at a time until he finally recovered. His mother, having given him up for dead, was crying when he came out of his delirium, and he heard her say, "I also wish to die if my son dies."

Sinkira knew what she meant. If he died, she would have nothing left for which to live. Already she had threatened suicide several times when things seemed more than she could bear. Sick as he was, Sinkira repeated some of the stories Kipkirir had told him about a loving Father and of His promises to help the poor people and those who suffer. He reminded her of the old man, who had now gone on his way, and asked, "Don't you believe perhaps the kind Father sent him just in time to help me get well? None of the villagers would help us."

Nentayia tried to believe what her son told her, and she begged, "Tell me more about this Father who is so strong. Does He really promise to help the poor and suffering? And does He do this without requiring an ox in return, as our *laibon* does?"

"Kipkirir told me this is true." Sinkira begged, "Won't you believe in this Jesus, and promise me that you will never hurt yourself? I myself believe in this kind, loving One, although I have not a great deal of knowledge about Him."

Nentayia promised, "I will give more thought to this Man who asks for no ox in return for His help. I will do nothing to harm myself if you ask it, my son."

Sinkira sighed in relief and slept.

But now the villagers treated him even more cruelly. If he displeased them they beat him, and often he crawled home bruised and bleeding after these encounters.

Most of the other village children attended school. But Sinkira could not go. He wanted to go to school more than anything else he could think of, but when he requested permission, the villagers replied, "No, you must herd the cattle."

Nemitil, his sister only five years older, constantly taunted him, while their grandmother told her, "If it weren't for Sinkira, your mother would have returned to her own village and we wouldn't have to be giving them any milk." Because of this, Nemitil blamed him for the extra work and took every opportunity to abuse him, yet she worked much less than he.

Konoi, their relative, threatened, "If you ever request to

go to school again I will beat you to death,'' and after some of the terrible beatings suffered at this man's hands, Sinkira didn't doubt for a moment that he meant every word, so he held his peace. In his heart he prayed to the God his friend talked about, ''Father, if You keep me alive, one day I will go to school too.''

During the dry season the grass grew so sparsely that the herd boy sometimes had to walk seven miles to find a grazing area for the cattle. He left the village early each morning after a breakfast of two glasses of milk—if he was fortunate.

Sinkira trudged over parched hills and across formerly verdant valleys, following the herd of cows and wishing for the rains to come and end the dry season. One day after traveling many miles with the cattle, he found a place near a trickling stream. The boy failed to notice the clouds gathering in the sky and scurrying across it as they joined with other clouds. By the time Sinkira, in the late afternoon, started the cattle on their way back to the village the sky was filled with ominous black clouds.

Hurriedly he attempted to get the cows started on their homeward way. But suddenly it seemed as if the heavens opened and the rain poured down, blotting from his sight the uncooperative cattle. Sinkira ran here and there trying to herd them toward the stream. However, at the stream that had once been a trickle of water he found a swollen river with a herd of elephants wallowing in the mud on the bank.

After much urging on his part, the cows finally went downstream a ways and began to cross over. But when the last cow was in the water, Sinkira began to worry about crossing himself. Certainly the stream was too swollen for him to walk through. He had not learned to swim. There was nothing for him to do but wait. He turned and walked away from the river and the herd of elephants. Soon he came to a hill, where he sat down and waited. He was not only thoroughly soaked but also cold. What should he do? He knew that although the rain should let up, the elephants could stay for hours at the muddy waters. For him to stay on the hill in the bush country would be extremely dangerous. Yet to cross over near the elephants would be even more dangerous!

Suddenly he remembered the stories that his friend had told him about the God who loves all people and who watches over all. Sinkira decided to pray to that God and ask for help.

After a short prayer for help, he stood up and began to shout while he waved his arms wildly. Within a short time he heard unfamiliar cow bells, and then saw Olemuyiangai, a herder, coming straight toward him. Sinkira shouted, "Be careful, the elephants! The elephants!"

Olemuyiangai stopped, followed a more circuitous route to the top of the hill, finally arriving where Sinkira sat huddled. He asked. "What are you doing up on this hill?"

Sinkira explained, "The elephants prevented me from crossing the river with my cattle. Now the cattle have gone on, and I don't know whether they went to the village or are lost, and I don't know what will happen to me when I return to the village."

Olemuyiangai sympathized, "I'm very sorry. What do you intend to do, now that the cows have gone on ahead of you and you are here alone?"

Sinkira, his head down and his arms folded about his knees, made no reply.

"Can you go with me to my village?" Olemuyiangai asked.

"No. The villagers will be very unhappy with me for not tending the cows properly. They would be even more angry if they learned that I went home with you to your village, so far from mine," responded Sinkira.

Olemuyiangai thought for a moment. Then he took Sinkara to the stream, picked up some very big sticks and beat them together. The noise frightened the elephants away.

Since the sun had long since set, this kind man helped Sinkira across the river and remained with him as he walked toward home through the dangerous bushy places.

When they neared the village, Sinkira said, "I'm all right now. I will be safe. I can run to the village alone from here and have no fear. Thank you for being so kind." He ran the rest of the way home, thanking the God of heaven for sending him help when he needed it most.

Stealthily he approached the village, expecting some reaction, either anger or concern. Instead, he discovered neither. The women were milking the cows, gossiping about the day's happenings. It relieved him to see the cows in the village, but he felt great disappointment that no one seemed to care about him. No one even greeted him as he ran past the village huts to his mother's.

When he reached his mother's hut, he found her in tears. Nentayia knew wild animals abounded in the bushes and that more than one herd boy never returned home.

"I'm all right," he assured her. "Again God sent help to me. The elephants at the crossing frightened the cows. But the cows all returned to the village, and then the God that Kipkirir told me about sent Olemuyiangai to help me."

Drying her tears, Nentayia whispered, "I thank Him that you are home safe."

After the rain came, grass became more abundant, and life became a bit easier. One day as Sinkira rested beneath a yellow fever tree, Konoi passed by on the trail. Upon seeing Sinkira resting, he shouted, "Why do you do nothing but sit under this tree? You are responsible for all these cows, yet you are sitting under a tree doing nothing!"

Grabbing hold of Sinkira's arm, he jerked him to his feet and began beating him with his stick. Too much *pombe*, perhaps, clouded his thinking, and he continued beating him until the boy finally dropped to the ground. Only then did Konoi leave, still furious.

Sinkira staggered home with difficulty that evening. His legs seemed made of rubber, his left shoulder drooped strangely, he ached and hurt all over, and black and blue places with bloody patches covered his entire body.

Nentayia cried, "Whatever happened to you?"

Sinkira sat down painfully and explained, "Konoi caught me resting in the shade while the cattle grazed nearby. He became very angry and beat me."

His mother felt over his body for possible broken bones, starting with his shoulder. He flinched as she carefully examined it; it appeared that the collar bone was the only bone broken, and there was nothing she could do about it. She could do nothing to avenge her son.

Sinkira with faith and confidence suggested, "Let's pray to God. He's with us."

However, Nentayia had too much hatred in her heart for Konoi and what he had done to her son to place her trust in some unknown God.

As the rainy season continued; the days loomed dark and foreboding, but the cattle needed to eat, so Sinkira, although his shoulder gave him much pain, set out early each morning with the cows, sometimes in the rain, sometimes between showers. The best grass grew across the river, and the cattle and Sinkira waded across the low places when rains hadn't been too heavy. He no longer needed to take them long distances from the river for good grazing. Now when he took the cattle out, he took a skin under which he huddled for cover in heavy downpours that often occurred during this time of the year.

Looking toward the Kisii Highlands, he could see the mountaintops shrouded in darkness, and then lightning flashed over them as the clouds poured out their accumulation of water. As he watched, Sinkira thought, "This is good. One day soon the grass will grow even greener and better than now."

Near evening Sinkira started the herd toward home.

When they reached the river, he realized once more he was in for trouble. Instead of the meandering, shallow stream they had crossed that morning, the rain again had changed it into a raging torrent. Many times the river had risen, but never had he seen it this angry and swollen, flooding beyond its banks, tearing trees and bushes out and taking them downstream. He urged the cattle, and after some hesitation, they plunged into the swift-flowing torrent and swam to the far side. Sinkira, now about seven, knew he would never be able to cross. Neither could he safely spend the night out in the bush, especially in this rain.

He watched anxiously as one after another of the cattle reached the far side, and finally there remained only one stubborn ox. Until now, Sinkira had watched with his head full of unhappy thoughts. But suddenly the idea popped into his head, "Why don't I just hold the tail of that ox? If it can swim across, I can float behind it."

Acting quickly, Sinkira grabbed the tail of the animal just as it stepped into the raging water. The huge animal began swimming strongly, seemingly unaware of Sinkira's presence. Looking a short distance downstream, Sinkira felt as if his heart almost stood still. He gripped the tail even tighter as he saw, instead of the smooth-flowing river he knew so well, the churning and foaming water of the rapids. He knew that if he should let go of that tail, the river would most certainly take him through the rapids, and he would be crushed on the rocks.

Quickly he looked away from the rapids, clutched the tail more tightly, and stared straight ahead toward the far side of the angry water and the welcome bank. The ox swam erratically, but eventually they made the far side. Sinkira let go the ox's tail and followed the animal home. As he walked he again thought about God and wondered, "Did God give me the thought to take hold of the ox's tail? If I hadn't, I would still be on the other side of the river with no way across. I must talk more to Kipkirir," he decided.

At home he told his mother about the experience and said, "I feel that the God of heaven must have told me what to do, or I should still be out there. Perhaps this is a good God."

"Something other than human must have been with you. We shall think some more about this God," Nentayia agreed.

She began doubting her old gods. Since Napangala's death, troubles had plagued her. So far her gods had done her no good. Sinkira appeared to believe in this new God, but something held Nentayia back.

By morning the flood of water had receded enough so that Sinkira took the cattle across the river to their favorite places to eat, and every day, sunshine or rain, Sinkira, hungry most of the time, spent with the ever-increasing herd of cattle, knowing that some of the villagers watched everything that he did. If he annoyed anyone, punishment would be swift and sure.

Nentayia sensed that life for Sinkira became more difficult with each passing day. How she hated to send him off in the morning with a half-filled stomach! Surely life couldn't go on like this for him forever. Yet, as she lay on her bed, she listened with open ears while the women gossiped as they went about their work. Whenever she heard Sinkira's name, she listened more intently.

One day she heard: "Did you know that Sinkira will be going with his cousin to the *manyatta* soon now?"

"No," another answered. "I wonder what Nentayia will do when he is gone?"

"Have no fear for her, but Sinkira will have a hard time pleasing that cousin of his."

This gossip gave Nentayia no joy whatsoever. The possibility of the villagers taking Sinkira from her had not occurred to her. What would happen to her if they took Sinkira away? Perhaps it was only idle gossip. She had heard such before. But soon her fear was realized.

Slave Boy at the *Manyatta*

Nentayia waited long and impatiently for Sinkira to come in one evening. Someone had given them a bit of maize, a big treat, and when his usual time to bring the cows back passed, her excitement changed into worry. She knew that many wild animals lurked in the dark. She also realized the hatred of many of the villagers, and as time passed, her fear turned into real anxiety.

At last he slipped into the dimly lit hut.

"My son, we have maize this evening," she began quickly. "You can make some porridge."

Sinkira grunted as he built the fire and put the pan with water on to heat. Even when he added the maize, Sinkira mumbled something to his mother, then fell silent.

The porridge bubbled in the pan. When it was ready they began eating. "My mother," Sinkira spoke up, "I have news that brings neither comfort nor joy to my heart."

"Umm," Nentayia answered.

In a whisper Sinkira confided, "I must go to the *manyatta* with a distant cousin. Only today he requested it."

Sinkira saw the pained look on his mother's face. She and Sinkira knew that "requested" amounted to a demand and that Sinkira had no choice. He would remain slave to this distant cousin until the *manyatta* was dismissed.

Tears ran down Nentayia's face as she tried to console her son, but this time the trouble would not go away, and not even his mother could soothe the fear Sinkira felt.

"My mother, how will you manage without anyone to look after you?" he asked. "I don't know when I can return even for a visit."

The days seemed longer and more full of trouble than ever. Word spread among the villagers about Sinkira and his distant cousin. Nentayia would be alone, because Sinkira would go as a slave to the *manyatta*. Nemitil, his sister, recently married, thought, "Now Sinkira will be away from the village for a long time." But her husband suggested, "Perhaps we should move in with your mother and take care of her while Sinkira is gone."

Reluctantly, Nemitil agreed, and they went to the hut and offered to take care of Nentayia. Sinkira felt a great burden fall from his young shoulders. Nothing could change Sinkira's dread of going as a slave to the *manyatta*, but he did feel better when he knew that his mother would have help. He spoke of this to Nentayia, "Nemitil's husband must be unusually kind. It is unheard of by Masai custom for a husband of a daughter to take care of his wife's mother."

"I have heard that he is a fine man." Nentayia nodded.

"Do you think that this God we wonder about told him to help us?"

"I know nothing of any god other than those we worship. If you know of another, perhaps He is helping us. Certainly something has helped you before," Nentayia conceded.

"Then if there is a God who cares for you, my mother, and I know He cares for me, perhaps going to the *manyatta* won't be so bad."

Nemitil and her husband had moved into the small hut of Nentayia before Sinkira left. The husband proved to be a kind man, and he treated Sinkira better than anyone other than his mother. Sinkira even hoped that Nemitil's attitude toward him had softened. Unfortunately, when her husband left for the day, her true feelings surfaced, and Sinkira spent as little time as necessary with her.

Sinkira knew about *manyattas,* and most boys were eager to go. Many of the younger boys went with their mothers to help care for an older brother. Going as a slave was different. Sinkira dreaded the day when he would be called. He continued herding the cattle but heard rumors that the *manyatta* place had been chosen, and he listened carefully to the conversations concerning the *manyatta*. All the young men from the last circumcision had gone into the bush following their time of confinement several months earlier. The *manyatta* must be ready for them to occupy when they returned.

The mothers of the boys built the *manyatta* far from the home village. Here their sons would live from three to five years learning to be adults, to take the responsibilities of governing themselves and their households when they married.

Mothers accompanied their sons if their husband had another wife, but if the husband had but one wife, the boys went without the help of their mothers and lived in huts with other boys also without their mothers. Any mother who went to the *manyatta* took her younger children with her, both boys and girls, and they helped with the chores to give the *moran* (boys who had been circumcised) more time to devote to the *laibon*, who governed the village.

As had always been, the mothers who came to the *manyatta* built huts for the boys. They were made of sticks tied together. The roof was flat, and the whole was covered with cow dung to make it waterproof. Each hut contained two rooms, one for the calves that the boys brought with them, and the other room for sleeping and kitchen quarters.

When the *manyatta* had been completed, the boys who had been in confinement came to the *manyatta*. This now would be their home for several years. Each boy had his cattle with him—cattle that he had received from relatives at the time of his tooth cutting, his ear cutting, or his more recent circumcision.

The way these boys or *moran* looked after their cattle partially showed whether they would be able to take care of a family when they married. However, since much of the time the *moran* would be out in the bush for various ceremonies, a herd boy was found to look after his cattle during the day.

At night the cattle returned to the gate that opened into the circle of huts, some of which joined at the ends, forming a corral, or *boma*. Sticks placed across the gate kept the cattle from wandering and also prevented prowlers from entering.

When Sinkira's cousin came for him to go to the *manyatta* as his slave, Sinkira did not resist. For the next several years it would be his lot to sleep in a hut with other herd boys, slaves like himself.

As soon as the *moran* were settled in the *manyatta*, the *laibon* and the elders chose a chief from among the *moran*. A great deal of responsibility accompanied the honor of being chosen as chief. At an impressive ceremony each *moran* presented the newly appointed chief with a bead which he strung on a cowhide thong and placed it around his neck as a sign of distinction. A long and beautifully decorated antelope horn was given to him, presented from one chief of the *manyatta* to the next. This was carried as a sign of great dignity. When the chief blew the horn, the sound carried far out into the bush as signal for all the *moran* to assemble for special meetings. His job included watching over all the other *moran*. He carried their complaints and requests to the *laibon* and brought back the *laibon's* response.

One laibon served as high chief, or president, as well as teacher and spiritual leader. He ruled this *manyatta* in his way, and no one dared question his methods. He taught these moran how to live a respectable Masai life when they returned to the village and he took his responsibilities very seriously. The *laibon* taught the *moran* to hunt and to fight, using some of the ancient techniques and adding a few of his own. Killing a lion brought the *moran* great honor. The *laibon* advised them when to go fight an enemy, or another tribe. If a young man wished to steal, he went to the *laibon* for strong medicine so that he wouldn't get caught.

Sinkira only observed as he lived at the *manyatta*. During the day he herded cattle. In the evening he rested and played. He noticed how the mothers prepared meals for themselves and the children, different from the milk, meat, and sometimes blood served to the *moran*. The *moran* diet was intended to make them strong and fearless. However, they treated their mothers with disrespect and never let the mothers see them eating, a practice which amazed Sinkira. He respected his mother and could never bring himself to mistreat her.

Sinkira, now seven or eight years old, thought of this as he tended the cattle each day. His stomach no longer complained of lack of food, although his diet was limited. His cousin expected and demanded a lot of him for so small a boy, and he endured many beatings at his hands.

Some time after the *manyatta* had been in session, Sinkira's cousin suggested that he go home to visit his mother.

Sinkira's heart felt light, and he was filled with happiness at the thought of seeing his mother again as he left the *manyatta*. It was a long distance to the village, but he knew the way well. As he approached a stream in a remote area, he heard a commotion ahead. The bushes grew so tall that he couldn't see over them, so he slipped nearer the stream and cautiously made his way toward the crossing. Upon reaching a clearing at the edge of the water, he peered through the bushes. There were many baboons washing themselves in the river, while others were playing in the trees nearby.

Fear welled inside him as he remembered stories of injuries inflicted even to adults by these large and dangerous animals. Sinkira's first instinct was to flee the scene. As yet he had been undetected by the baboons; even the hoary-haired grandfather standing guard over the many frolicking animals hadn't seen him. He tried to run. Then suddenly his heart went out again to God. It had been such a long time since he had seen his mother, and he had no idea whether his cousin would again give him permission to go. Baboons or not, he ran until he found a small flat place near the bank of the river, above the place where the baboons bathed. He picked up a large stone. Walking quietly now, fearful they would smell him, he found a place to hide in the undergrowth. He waited and watched. The baboons appeared to be undisturbed, so he heaved the stone with all his might. The splash surprised them all, even the one standing guard. Sinkara shouted.

Had the baboons known that the enemy was only a small, frightened boy, their reaction might have been different. They hurriedly splashed out of the river and swung through the trees, screaming baboon obscenities and clearing out in record time. After waiting to see whether they would return, Sinkira crossed the stream easily and remembered to thank this wonderful God that Kipkirir had told him about—the God who had shown him what to do.

He entered the village undetected and went to the door of the hut. "My mother!" he called.

Nentayia turned in her bed. Sinkira saw tears well up in her eyes as she cried, "My son," she asked, "you are well?"

"Yes, Mother, I am well. I have a few days to spend with you before having to go back to the *manyatta,*" Sinkira told her.

"Does your cousin treat you well?" his mother asked.

"If I don't displease him, I do all right," Sinkira answered.

"You no longer lack food, my son. How you have grown!" A smile came over her wrinkled face.

"Yes, we do have food to eat, and women to cook it for

us. But what about you, Mother? Are you well? Do they treat you kindly and give you enough to eat?" he asked.

Before she could respond, a shadow darkened the door and Nemitil entered the hut. "What are you doing here, you good-for-nothing boy?" she shouted.

Sinkira no longer shrank from her when she shouted at him, but he answered her politely, "I have but a few days to visit with my mother and then I must return to the *manyatta*."

Before she had time to respond her husband entered, and he greeted Sinkira warmly. "Do they treat you well?" he asked.

"Yes, they take care of me," Sinkira responded.

Nemitil crossed the small room to Nentayia's bed, and Sinkira sensed from the way she cared for her that his mother had softened Nemitil's heart. That made the long journey worthwhile. He had always wondered whether his mother was receiving good care. Now he felt better. Nemitil really seemed to care for the bed-ridden woman.

After the brief time home, Sinkira returned to the drudgery of being a *manyatta* slave. He received no warm welcome when he went back. The next day he once more went out to herd the cattle of his cousin. His only enjoyment came in the evenings when the *moran* sat around the fire, bragging of what they had accomplished during the day; at least now his stomach felt satisfied.

He learned many things by watching and listening. Early at the *manyatta* he had learned that the less he asked, the less punishment he received. He learned much about the value of their cattle. The cattle were bled each day, but while blood was considered essential to a good diet for strength and bravery, they drew blood from different cattle at different times. The blood was drawn by tying a rope around the neck of the animal, causing the vein to stand out like a small rope. Then a special arrowhead was shot into the vein. Upon removing the arrowhead, the blood poured out, which they caught in a special gourd. When the amount of blood needed was taken, the rope was untied and the bleeding soon stopped.

The women took the gourd and prepared the blood for the *moran*. Sometimes they drank it plain, but usually they stirred it with a stick, separating and settling it before skimming off the clots and mixing the rest with milk.

When the *moran* told the herd boys to take the cows to the salt lick some distance from the *manyatta*, they accompanied them to watch for lions. Two or three herd boys by themselves could not possibly protect several hundred cattle.

Before Sinkira went to the *manyatta*, his cousin's mother had made him an *olchuret*, a large, heavy cow skin he used as an umbrella to shelter him from heavy rains. Usually the boys tied their *olchurets* to the back of an ox or a cow. The *olchuret* had a strong handle so the older and stronger boys could carry it and have it with them when they needed it.

One day Sinkira put his on the back of a cow, tied it with a strong leather thong, and started for the grazing place. During the day it began to rain heavily. He took the *olchuret* from the cow's back and attempted to cover himself with it. The storm increased, and the cattle wandered about in search of a sheltered place. He tried to keep them together, but each went a different way. As the rain beat down, the *olchuret* became heavier. Finally Sinkira could carry it no longer. He took it off and dragged it on the path behind him as he went after his herd.

With the huge *olchuret* dragging, he couldn't see anything behind him in the path. At last the rain began to abate, but as it let up somewhat, he heard a voice behind him shout, "Sinkira! Sinkira!" Sinkira looked around. To his horror he saw a hyena following just a few yards away.

One of the *moran* suddenly appeared and chased the hyena away. "You can thank your God, little boy, because He saved your life. Otherwise you would have been eaten by the hungry hyena,'' the *moran* said. He then helped Sinkira collect the cattle and drive them back to the *manyatta*.

Sinkira pondered the words of the *moran*. What did he know about this God?

At last the time when the *manyatta* would be dismissed drew near. As Sinkira listened, each evening now the *moran* talked in hushed tones. One said, "I am one of the lucky ones. My mother has more than one son. They won't choose me."

Usually the *moran* outdid one another trying to be chosen for some honor. Another whispered, "But I'm the only son of my mother. What if they choose me?"

Sinkira and a friend discussed these strange bits of conversation. They remembered the tradition of choosing two *moran* to bear the sins of all. These two must be only sons, exceptionally good *moran*, and worthy of such a serious burden. No one wanted to be chosen for this honor, as it meant an early death and heavy burdens to bear, with the sins of all the *moran* resting on their shoulders.

The elders and *laibon* considered carefully. Even the usual braggarts kept their silence as this council met to choose the two most worthy of the responsibilities. Some, with other brothers, didn't appear concerned. But even they held their peace as this important meeting progressed. Many *moran* must be considered.

One evening the *moran* appeared more quiet than usual. Most of them, especially only sons, retired early. There were no stories told around the fire that night. Sinkira also went to bed earlier than usual. As he lay there waiting for sleep to come, he could almost feel the horror he would feel if his name were being considered. How horrible for the two whose names should be chosen as the *olotuno* and the *oloburuengene!*

It seemed as if he had just dropped off to sleep when screaming and yelling in the *manyatta* center roused him. He crept to the door of the hut, peered into the semidarkness, and watched as the elders dragged a young man out of a hut near his. The young man fought wildly. His relatives rushed from the hut to help him, but in spite of all they could do, he disappeared into the conference hut. Across the way Sinkira saw another *moran* being half-dragged, half-carried, screaming, toward the same hut. He also fought savagely, injuring one of the elders badly. No relatives went to his aid, and he, too, finally disappeared into the conference hut.

Sinkira crawled miserably back to his bedroll, sickened by what he had seen and still hearing the screaming of the desperate young *moran* ringing in his ears. He dared not go watch, nor did he care to do so. The first one had been especially good to Sinkira, and he wondered what would happen to him now.

According to Masai custom, these two *moran* who had been chosen and dragged from their huts were now eternally lost, because they must bear all the sins of the entire *manyatta* since its beginning, and they knew that the sins were many and terrible. Before the elders dismissed them, they blessed each one and suggested, "You should now marry early, as soon as you can, and have children, preferably men-children to carry on your name, because you will not have as many years to live as some of the other *moran*."

The following day the elders gave each of the two *moran* a cow as an addition to his herd, and all the other *moran* gathered in the center of the village, and each removed two of his black beads and gave one to each of the chosen two. The elders strung these beads on a thin, strong piece of cow cartilage, and the chosen two, the *olotuno* and *oloburuengene*, must wear these beads at all times.

Now that they had been chosen, Sinkira noticed that the other young *moran* now respected these two who had been chosen because they had proven themselves to be greater than most. If any of the other *moran*, either before or after they left the *manyatta*, did something to annoy the two chosen, they removed a bead, spoke that moran's name who had annoyed them, and placed a curse on him saying, "Now he will die."

However, as time passed, when a *moran* died who had placed a bead upon the strands worn by the *olotuno* and the *oloburuengene,* that *moran's* bead would be removed. The sins were gone.

Now the days were filled with preparations for the *manyatta* dismissal. Sinkira brought the cattle in one evening and found a small hut being built in the center of the enclosure. The *moran* considered it to be holy. Built smaller than the huts used as living quarters, it appeared different, too, like a place set apart for a specific purpose. Sinkira knew what that purpose would be, and his heart felt great joy as he realized that soon he would be free once more.

In the center of this hut the elders placed a certain stick they considered to be holy, taken from a holy tree, and planted it like a flag pole. The council of elders chose girls, virgins without any blemish, to smear the hut with cow dung. These girls were to care for the hut until time for dismissal.

The elders again met in the council hut and began considering the name of each *moran*. "Now what do you know about Lemashon? Do you think he is worthy?" asked one of the elders.

"Lemashon cannot be trusted to take care of his family. He goes without telling anyone; he takes what he wants when he sees something. No, I don't think Lemashon should be allowed to enter the sacred hut."

"Now I think that Olokonoi is a good *moran*. He helps when there is a need, and he has done good things for me."

"But did you know that he committed fornication with Netniana on several occasions?"

"So that is why he tried to make me think he was so good! No, he is not fit to enter the hut if he did that."

The elders took a long time to deliberate, and no one outside of the council knew their decisions. With many elders watching as the *moran* went through the *manyatta,* few sins had gone unnoticed.

All the strengths and weaknesses of each *moran* were discussed. As the elders were deliberating, the *moran* began remembering things done that they hoped no one knew about or that would be forgotten, so they became very serious and most concerned.

The elders made a list of all those who had made serious mistakes, who had been scarred in battle with the enemy, who had lost an eye or even a tooth. People with names on this list would not be allowed to enter the sacred hut. When they emerged from their council hut, the elders called the *moran* together, took them to the river to a place of white soil, and began decorating their bodies with the white clay.

Sinkira could not be near when this went on, as the cattle needed to graze, and some days the walk took him far from the *manyatta*, but he saw them that evening when he returned the cattle to their owners. The marks looked strange to him. No two were alike, and no one could tell whether the marks showed honor or disgrace. However, the elders knew what the white markings on the faces, legs, and arms meant, and the most impressive appeared on those who had killed an enemy in battle or a lion.

Now the *moran* were making plans to leave their *manyatta* village, their home of five years. Probably they would return to their home village the following week. Sinkira asked questions of various herd boys and finally found one who had not been out that day and could tell him what had happened.

"After the *moran* were decorated at the river, they ran as fast as they could, racing for the sacred hut," he told Sinkira. "They knew that to enter the sacred hut and be blessed would be the crowning glory of their years at the *manyatta*. However, they found elders guarding the entrance."

When his friend hesitated, Sinkira asked breathlessly, "Then what happened? Please, tell me what happened then?"

So the friend went on. "The elders could tell by the markings whether the moran could enter, and as each *moran* approached the sacred hut, if the markings showed that he had committed some sin, the elders refused to allow him into the hut. Sinkira, you should have seen some of them fight to get past the elders!"

"Do I know any of the ones who didn't get in? Let me guess. I don't think they would have let Olemeyioloi in."

"No, he didn't get in, but he fought and knocked one of the elders to the ground. But other elders moved to the doorway, and Olemeyioloi didn't get in. He is still angry about it."

"He should have known they wouldn't allow him to enter!"

"He hoped his wicked deeds would be forgotten. The markings are secret so none of the *moran* knew when they ran for the sacred hut whether they were marked to go in or were rejected. Olemeyioloi is terribly ashamed, even though he put up a good fight. Look out for him tonight! He and the others who were turned away are now considered either sinful or cowardly.

"But, Sinkira, those who did enter do something very strange. My brother got in, and he told me that they must kneel down, as though in prayer, and that the girls pour over their bare backs a mixture of milk, honey, and urine of the cow. For added show of strength and bravery, the girls added a fire ant—you know—the kind of ant that clusters together. They are tiny, but do you remember how terrible their bite hurts? And those warriors are not to utter a sound or appear to feel the bites of those horrible ants!"

"Did any of the *moran* show cowardice when they got in?"

"No, they all stayed inside until the elders let them go.

My brother told me that the *laibon* blessed the *moran* that passed the test and allowed them to return to their huts. He told me how wonderful he felt, full of peace and pride."

"I'm so glad that your brother ended his days at the *manyatta* with pride. He will make a good elder," Sinkira remarked, thoughtfully.

Time went slowly for Sinkira now. Each day he hoped to be able to return to his mother's village, but eight days passed before the *laibon* officially released both the *moran* and the others living in the *manyatta*. At the end of eight days, the *moran's* heads were shaved of the long hair grown since entering the *manyatta*. Each one then returned to his father's hut to await another ceremony before being awarded the name of elder, or *ilpayiani*. During this time, they were to continue to control their appetites, still eating their meat without salt and drinking milk and blood. Many found it more difficult to control themselves when away from the *manyatta,* yet it must be done. Masai customs dictated it.

Sinkira felt relief when his cousin relieved him of his duty as a herd boy. He received no thanks, nor did he expect any. He had performed his duties well and had eaten amply, and that was thanks enough, so far as his cousin was concerned.

As he started the journey home, he had grave forebodings concerning his future. The one time he had returned home during the *manyatta*, Nemitil had made it perfectly clear that she did not want Sinkira around. She had shown her hatred of him in many ways, by cruel little things she had said and by beating him if he had displeased her in any way. He hadn't seen much of the other villagers during that brief visit so didn't know how they would receive him. He did know that, having been a slave boy in the *manyatta,* his status would be even lower than before.

Sinkira pondered these things as he walked the long way home. As he neared the village, wonderful feelings of love welled up inside him for his mother, yet a terrible fear of the future lurked inside his mind. It occurred to him at one point that he might not even have a future. More than one of the villagers had threatened his life before he went to the *manyatta*. Once more his mind turned to the God of whom he knew so little. "Only You know what will happen to me, God," he prayed as he entered his home village.

Home Again!

When Sinkira went into his mother's hut, he found her lying on her bed. He took her gnarled hand in his and saw the tears come into her eyes as she looked up into his face. For a few moments neither could speak. It had been almost five years since Sinkira's last visit.

Nemitil came into the hut and found her brother and mother there. At once she began to demand him to do many demeaning chores. She beat him and yelled at him while he tried to accomplish what she had asked him to do. "You lazy one," she screamed. "You have no sense in your head. We did very well without you. Go back to your job of herding the cattle."

That year the rainy season was shorter than usual. Soon the grass turned brown, and it became harder for Sinkira to find grazing land for the cattle. Each day he took them farther and farther from the village.

When he returned one evening from herding the cows, Nemitil's husband remarked, "We must move or all our cattle will die of hunger."

Preparations for the move were not elaborate. There were few household goods to be moved. They made a crude stretcher on which to carry Nentayia, for she could not walk. The trip over the rough trail was not easy for her, Sinkira knew, for she often cried out as they jostled the stretcher as they traveled over rough places.

Sinkira felt little or no regret when they left the village.

He wondered, as they trudged along, mile after weary mile, if Nemitil would ever soften her attitude toward him.

When they arrived at the new location, they immediately set about to build two huts, one for Nemitil, her husband, and two children, and another nearby for Sinkira and Nentayia. No bed graced this hut. The one made for Nentayia by Napangala had remained in the deserted hut in the old village, and Nentayia now slept on a mat on the floor, as most Masai do.

Nemitil still cared for her mother, leaving more time for Sinkira to be away with the cattle. Sinkira often thought, "Nemitil hates me so much, but she loves our mother. For that I am happy, and, therefore, I can bear much of her abuses to me."

It appeared that Sinkira had been released from one slavery to be trapped in another. At the *manyatta* he had had all he needed to eat. But now any food was difficult to get. All of them knew hunger. And as a growing boy, Sinkira's stomach complained most of the time.

Each day as he herded the cattle and did the other chores demanded of him, he talked with the God he only knew from stories told him by Kipkirir, his little village friend. He often prayed, "Please, God, show me what to do. This is no life for me."

Grazing improved after their move, and he needed less time to reach the preferred grasses, but Sinkira found it gave him more time to think. He began to miss other boys his age, and to his surprise, he even missed the old village. Though some of the elders had mistreated him, yet he had had some friends his own age. Especially he missed Kipkirir, the one who had told him about Jesus, the God who cared for everyone, even little boys who were poor. He wished he could learn more about this Jesus man. But there was no one to tell him.

One day the family saw a figure in the distance and soon recognized Konoi, a relative from their home village. He saw the fine grazing conditions and liked what he saw. They flooded him with questions about their old village friends. "All are hungry," he said. "Cattle are thin and dying. Water is far away and difficult to carry enough for drinking. You are well to be here."

Not long after the visit, Konoi brought his family to the new grazing area. Soon other villagers followed, until they had built another village around the two small huts, that of Nemitil and her husband, and Nentayia and Sinkira.

This meant more cattle to graze the same land, and Sinkira now faced another problem. Until now he herded where he pleased and allowed the cattle to wander where they wished. Now he shared this abundant countryside with others, and soon grazing nearby vanished, forcing Sinkira to take his herd ever farther from the village to find green grass.

The meadows were scattered among thick thorn bushes. Sometimes the cattle grazed among the bushes, which made it difficult for Sinkira, who needed to keep an eye on all of them constantly. Sinkira chased after one cow and then another. The tough hides of the cattle scarcely felt the thorns, but as Sinkira ran through them, the long thorns appeared to reach for him, tearing his sheet. Many evenings he returned with his legs scratched and bleeding.

One day several of the cattle wandered from the herd and started through the bush in search of better grass. He followed them, attempting to drive them back to the rest of the herd. As he walked through the thorny bushes, he saw what appeared to be one of the villager's dogs, lying between the shrubs.

As Sinkira approached the animal, he called, "Simba, Simba, Simba," the name given the dog because it resembled a lion, which is called *simba* by the Masai. Sinkira got no response. "Strange," he thought. Simba always came to him when he called. He stopped and stared at the animal for some time. It still looked like Simba, but something seemed to tell him, "Maybe this is a lion!"

Suddenly, he realized the terrible mistake he had almost made. This animal's muscles bulged, and he clearly saw it was a huge lion. As he watched, he saw the lion's tail begin to twitch ever so slightly. He thought, "This lion is going to attack me! What shall I do?"

Should he go back to the other cattle and let the few go on their way? But he knew the beating he would get if he should be caught neglecting his duty. "I'll just go ahead and see what is going to happen," he decided. Keeping his eyes on the lion, he slowly approached the huge cat resting beside the path.

The lion didn't move, except for the tail twitching slowly as Sinkira passed in the pathway. As soon as he left the lion behind, he ran to catch up with the wandering cows. He found them easily, but to return to the herd meant passing the same way, and to Sinkira's horror, the lion still lay beside the path.

The cows saw the lion on their return, and Sinkira had to constantly prod them along until they passed it. Sinkira passed within a few yards of the lion, and again it only stared at him. When he returned the straying cows to the herd, he collapsed with fear and then began to scream. "Help! Please, help me!"

People from another village heard his cries and went to see about the commotion he was causing. Finally finding Sinkira huddled on the ground in fear, they asked, "What is the trouble, little boy?"

"There is a lion around here!" Sinkira trembled but jumped up and went to the place where he had seen the lion. But it had slipped away into the bush.

When the villagers saw the footprints of the lion, they said, "This was a large lion, little boy. Why didn't it hurt you?" Sinkira couldn't answer them. Could the God of Kipkirir again have protected him?

Often Sinkira remembered this experience when things went badly at home, and he wondered whether God had once more saved his life. "If God could take care of me when a lion could have eaten me, surely He will take care of me again," he thought.

By the time Sinkira reached the age of twelve, it was time for the special ear-cutting ceremony. All Masai children knew about it.

Sinkira said little as the preparations for the ceremony were made. He thought a lot about it though. He remembered well the last time the children had endured this ordeal. He remembered the pus oozing down their necks when infection set in after the ear cutting. He remembered the sticks put through the hole made in the ear lobe, beginning with smaller ones and progressing to ever-larger ones. He also knew that some of the crueler children would deliberately slip up behind another and jerk the ear, pulling off the entire ear lobe.

Knowing that their time would eventually come, many of the children experimented with much smaller holes. Even Sinkira, himself, had made some tiny holes in his ear lobes to see how it felt. He didn't like it—in fact, he made a secret vow. In spite of the fact that he thought that some of the girls in particular did look exceptionally beautiful with their ear lobes long enough to touch their shoulders, and also in spite of the fact that this was another time for the giving of gifts to the children, he determined that no one would ever cut his ear. No one. Not ever!

The time for the ceremony arrived. The cutting specialist arrived, and the children were taken to the village center—Sinkira along with the others. He stood back and watched as the specialist cut ear after ear, someone else inserted the stick, all the while the child dared not utter a sound. Everyone cheered for them and gave each child gifts of goats, sheep, or cows.

Sinkira tried to slip away before his turn came, but an elder tried to stop him. Defiantly he said, "I refuse to have my ears cut." Then pulling out a knife he threatened, "If anyone tries to cut my ears, I will cut him with this knife. And if you try to catch me later, I will use either this knife or an *orinka* [club]."

The elder stepped back in astonishment. No Masai child had ever spoken with such lack of respect. However, Sinkira left the ceremony untouched. This ceremony appeared to him an evil thing, and he wanted no part of it.

Of course his refusal to have a part in the ceremony created embarrassment for the entire family. Children began to shout at him, "You are a cowardly hyena!" The talk among the elders hurt the family even more. "That boy shows no respect," said one.

"Yes, he threatened to cut me. Have you ever heard of such a thing?" agreed the elder who had let him go.

"He should be punished severely," added a third.

Nemitil felt she could take no more. "Sinkira is not only a cowardly hyena, but lazy. He has embarrassed us at both the tooth and ear-cutting ceremonies. No one gave him any gifts. When I get through with him, he'll be sorry!" she muttered. And now life became even more miserable for the young lad.

Because of the pain and suffering of his friends after the ceremony, Sinkira looked after the herds of some of the other boys while they recovered. The cattle were unaccustomed to feeding together, and when Sinkira returned them to the village each evening, he was extra tired. But he saw many of his friends suffering from the cuttings, some with infected wounds. Sinkira stumbled toward his hut wondering, "For what are these boys and girls suffering? Of what value is having the ear cut?" Then upon reaching the hut, he endured the cruel words and more chores his sister had for him. When finally he wrapped himself in his body-sheet and lay down he fell asleep immediately—but morning always came too soon.

One day Konoi, Sinkira's distant relative and enemy, caught him in the bush, far from the village. He gave him such a thrashing that his body swelled all over. When he dragged himself home that evening, Nentayia said, "You must go away. Konoi told another that he plans to beat you to death next time. It is their plan to take what little property we have left. You must leave, because it is too much for you to bear."

Sinkira knew that his mother spoke the truth concerning Konoi and his intentions. "Where shall I go, my mother?" he asked.

Driven From Home

Where should Sinkira go? Nentayia had given this much thought as she lay upon her mat. "You can escape to the land of the Kipsigis, or you could go to the land of the white settlers. It would be closer if you could reach the settlements near Sotik, in the land of the Kipsigis. You could get a job. You have learned to work hard. Just go there for safety. I will miss you, but I want you to live, not die."

"How do I get to this place—this Sotik?" he asked.

"Actually, it is very far. But it is better than staying here. Because Konoi is planning to kill you, you must go soon," Nentayia told him, trying to hide her fears.

"My mother, I will leave soon and find work," Sinkira promised.

Early one morning before the cocks started crowing, he crept out of the tiny hut and slipped into the darkness. He headed toward the Sotik Highlands. No one would miss him, except his mother—of that he felt sure. There would be all kinds of wild animals hiding in the bush as he walked along, and he kept a watchful eye for lions, hyenas, and elephants. Just how long his journey would take, he had no idea. His thoughts now were for the future. What would it hold for a Masai boy in disgrace by his own villagers?

He walked until about noon, when he came to a boundary of the Kisiis, Kipsigis, and the Masai territory. In the distance he saw some people but decided against meeting them. Sinkira turned toward a stream. He was thirsty after his long morning walk. However, some boys he saw in the distance, saw him and sent their dogs after him.

The dogs loomed huge as they lunged toward him. He heard their vicious barking, and he turned and raced back the way he had come—back up the hill. He didn't stand a chance against the speed of the dogs.

They came closer and closer. Sinkira looked around for some bush to hide behind or a tree to climb. To his horror, he realized there were neither bushes nor trees in this area. Without even a thought, he sent up a silent prayer for help and then turned to face the dogs.

"Get away from me," he commanded. "Sa, Sa, Sa!" That meant to go on ahead of him, a sound dogs who herd animals understand. The dogs passed him, one on either side. They continued running up the hill.

As he saw them pass him, Sinkira felt a sensation that he didn't understand. He tingled all over in a feeling of relief, and he started thinking happy thoughts. "Those dogs could have killed me, and no one would have helped me," he realized.

Once again this God, whom he didn't really know, had intervened and saved his life. He breathed a prayer of thanks and began singing some of the songs Kipkirir had taught him in the evenings around the fire in the village years ago. He remembered many things Kipkirir told him, and he decided it must have been God who told him to say, "Sa, Sa, Sa." No one else cared whether he lived or died!

Sinkira rested a while after this scare, then continued his journey. After going a short distance he found a high, strong barbed-wire fence. He could find no way through, so just followed it down farther and farther, until he came to a strong metal gate. But he found that a large padlock secured the gate.

Now what should he do? How could he go through? He sat down to rest a few minutes. Then a thought occurred to him—"Why don't you just push it?"

Acting upon this idea, he pushed the gate, and it swung open. As he walked through it he wondered, "What happened? How can this be?" Fear seized him. If a watchman found him, he could be in serious trouble. Yet, he saw no one as he hurried down to the farmhouse.

Suddenly he saw many people going to their homes. His stomach growled hungrily. The farm workers were going home for their lunches. It seemed an eternity to Sinkira since he had had his glass of milk before he had left the village.

To his delight, he discovered some Masai in the group of people who now passed him. He greeted them in Masai, and one of them recognized him.

"What are you doing so far from your village?" one asked. "Will no one miss you?" He finally invited Sinkira to go in to lunch with him. The man knew some of Sinkira's family, so he asked, "Why did you leave your village? What do you plan to do now?"

"The people in my village hate me because my father died in battle before I was born," Sinkira began. "My mother remained in his village. Because they now want to kill me, I must leave my village and find work in order to live."

"You are too young to work on this farm," the man said. "But there are other farms nearby."

After eating, Sinkira rested. That night he slept in the hut with the Masai family. In the morning, his new friend suggested, "You are still much too exhausted to go on. Why not stay another day with us and rest?"

Sinkira accepted, and the following morning, the Masai gave Sinkira directions to another farm where he might find work.

Sinkira started out, scuffling his bare feet along the dusty road. Certainly it was easier than traveling across country had been a couple of days before! The place to which the Masai directed him was still a long distance away, about thirty kilometers, and he walked four hours without a rest.

As the sun rose higher in the sky, heat waves rose from the hot roadbed ahead of him, and Sinkira rested a few minutes in the shade of a thorn tree.

Once more he started out. Soon he came upon a man mending a punctured bicycle tube. Sinkira's eyes opened wide at the sight of the bicycle. Never had he seen such a machine.

"Little boy, can you help me?" the man asked, stopping his work to talk to Sinkira.

Sinkira for a moment stood speechless. Then he nodded and began to help the man.

"I am going to the village of Nyaronde. A kind man told me that there might be work for a boy my age in that village," Sinkira responded.

When the bicycle tube was repaired and the tire was back on the bicycle, the man offered Sinkira a ride the rest of the way to the farm near the village. How Sinkira wished his mother could see him riding in style on a bicycle.

All too soon for Sinkira they arrived at the farm and the kind man left him by the roadside. The young lad felt very lonely. He spoke very poor Ekugusii and Kipsigis. How would he fare?

As he stood by the road wondering what to do, a man who appeared to be a Masai approached him. Sinkira greeted him in Masai. With great relief, Sinkira learned that the man was not only a Masai but was on his way to the same farm Sinkira had been told to go to for work. The two walked to the labor camp together.

The man invited Sinkira to his home. He asked many questions. He had come from another village himself, so he knew none of the villagers from Sinkira's village. But as is the custom of the Masai, Sinkira was welcomed into the home, and the man promised to do all he could to help. He told Sinkira that he knew of some boys working on this farm. This gave Sinkira hope.

The next morning Sinkira's new friend offered him some

breakfast before leaving to go to the farm manager to see about a job for Sinkira.

The day passed slowly. Why didn't the man come back for him so he could finally go to work? Sinkira wondered.

The man returned in the afternoon. Sinkira could tell from the expression on his face that he had found no work for him. He explained that there was no work for such a little fellow as Sinkira, but he suggested he try at the tea plantation down the road.

"What is a tea plantation?" Sinkira asked.

"Many tea plants grow there—as far as your eye can see are tea plants. Boys pick the tea leaves from the top of the plants; then the leaves are put out to dry. There are many Masai boys working there. Why don't you go there to look for work? You could pick tea leaves." The man paused. Then seeing the discouraged look on Sinkira's face he said, "If you wait with us for three days a tractor will be driving to the plantation. I can get a ride on it for you, if you want to go that way."

A tractor! Sinkira had seen them only from a distance, but if it meant staying with this kind family three days and not having to walk alone, he would chance riding on this huge machine that made so much noise! Sinkira agreed. He spent the time looking over the farm and getting extra rest, which he so badly needed. Best of all, he ate with this family—a blessing indeed to the hungry, growing boy.

The tractor arrived in three days just as the man predicted. A wide-eyed Sinkira proudly rode on the tractor the rest of the way to the Sotik Highlands, where the tea plantations were situated, just beyond Sotik Town.

They arrived in the late evening, and Sinkira met many boys. To his disappointment, these Masai boys were all grown-up. Only about three years older than Sinkira; they appeared much older to him because he was small for his age.

They greeted him kindly and told him of various jobs on

the plantation. One said, "Some hoe in the gardens." Another said, "Yes, but most of us pick tea leaves. But I don't think you can do that—you are too small to lean over the plants to find the tender leaves."

"But I need work badly and I think I can do it," Sinkira protested.

They agreed to take him to the manager the next morning, knowing well that the manager would say No.

The manager looked Sinkira over from his bare head to his bare feet and asked why he thought he could pick tea leaves. Sinkira answered, "I know they say the tea plants are too high for me to reach over and the basket is large and heavy, but I'm accustomed to hard work. No one will know until I try. Won't you at least let me try before saying No?"

The manager smiled at Sinkira and decided to place him on a trial basis. He gave him the measuring stick to see whether the tea plants were tall enough to pick the leaves, and a large basket to be worn on his back, and intended to reach to the waist.

Poor Sinkira! When he put the basket on, it reached well below his hips, but instead of giving up, he thought, "I'll try to carry this big basket in my hands until I get to the tea bushes, and then I'll see what I can do."

He felt ridiculous as he carried, and then dragged the huge basket through the tea fields. He found the bushes that were up to the waists of the other workers, up to his neck. He struggled through the rows, pushing bushes aside as the basket caught, and when he reached the place where he was to begin picking, he tried to figure out a way to pick the tea leaves.

"I'm sorry, but I just can't do it," he told the manager during the lunch break. "Thank you for letting me try. The bushes are too high for me yet."

The older Masai boys felt a kinship to this likable, determined boy, for they suggested that he go to a dairy farm nearby and ask for a job.

"Can you herd cattle?" one asked.

"Why don't you stay here with us for a while," one of the boys suggested.

For a month Sinkira stayed with his new friends. At the end of the month, about twenty Masai boys left to look for some other work. All of them were at least six feet tall, and they quite dwarfed Sinkira, but they invited him to go along with them, as they wandered from farm to farm for several days seeking employment.

A few of the older boys found employment; others became weary, and when they spotted a camp for Masai and other tribes, they stayed for the night. By morning they had reached a decision and approached Sinkira, "It seems that when we go in a large group like this, we cannot be employed on a farm. It would be better to scatter. Since you are younger, you must not accompany us. We don't want you any longer."

Sinkira knew how discouraged they must feel.

Once more Sinkira found himself alone, going from one farm to another, asking managers for work—any kind of work—and receiving the same answer each time, "We have no work for a boy as young as you."

Finally he reached the forest with areas cleared for farms here and there. Stopping at the labor camp of the next farm, he found some men sipping *pombe* through bent reeds. In fact, there were many adults there, and when they saw this poor urchin standing in the doorway, they called out, "Welcome, boy."

He learned that these men were Kipsigis. He understood enough of their language by now so that he could communicate with them, and they offered him a chair, some food, and some *pombe*.

The farm manager sadly told Sinkira that there was no work for him there. "Little boy, I'm sorry, but we have no work for anyone as young as you." Then he added quickly, "But let us bless you as you go on your way that God will provide work for you somewhere." The men gathered around Sinkira, poured a mixture of *pombe* and milk on his head, and blessed him, saying, "May you have good luck and good health."

Sinkira sadly left. This time he had no direction in particular to go. He traveled until around noon. Then coming to a small stream he knelt down to drink deep draughts of the cool water before continuing on his way.

The sun shone down on him unmercifully. Beads of perspiration gathered and began to run down his face, neck, and back. His old sheet, the only clothing he owned, hung damp and clammy on his thin body. His mind wandered back to Nentayia. He hoped Nemitil treated her well, now that he had run away. Would she blame her and make things worse for his mother? This running away was not fun and games. Finding work was much more difficult than he had thought.

He knew that to return home would mean almost certain death, so he staggered ever onward, avoiding the hot roadbed. Even as he sent up a silent prayer, he began to wonder about this God who supposedly loved and cared for him. Would He desert him now, at his greatest time of need?

On His Own

The heat of the road caused mirages to float and hover, giving a feeling of unreality. First a lake appeared, only to disappear. Then a grove of trees and grass, indicating water, appeared, and again, when he reached it, he found it had moved on down the road ahead of him.

Hearing a noise behind him, he turned and saw a man rapidly approaching in a cloud of dust. The man on a bicycle stopped and greeted him in Kipsigis. "You look very tired and sweaty, do you not?"

"Yes, I'm very tired and hot," Sinkira answered in broken Kipsigis. "I've been walking all day looking for a job. Now I'm going to a certain mango farm a friend told me about. It is a long way yet, but I must keep going."

The man understood Sinkira's poor Kipsigis and offered him a ride.

"Sir, I appreciate that!" Sinkira responded.

So he rode again on a bicycle all the way to the mango farm. Sinkira trudged to the camp, where he saw some boys playing outside. He sat down near them, and soon they walked over to greet him. The boys seemed to realize immediately that he was a Masai, and one of them went for his father.

"Are you in good health?" the man greeted him in Masai fashion.

"Greatly, but I do need help," responded Sinkira.

"Why are you here alone, little boy?"

Sinkira told the story about leaving home and the hard time he had had looking for work.

As they visited, the girls brought supper outside for the boys and included food for Sinkira. He relished every bite, and while they ate, the father returned to the house and ate with his wife and daughters. After filling Sinkira's gnawing cavity, the family invited him to spend the night with their sons.

In the morning the boys said, "We know of a place where there is a job for a little fellow like you. Let us go to the place, and we will introduce you to the manager who can give you a job to do."

After breakfast they set off. They took Sinkira to the office, and to his surprise, he found the father of the boys in whose home he had slept the night before. Only then did Sinkira discover that he had gone to the home of the manager of a farm. "Why did this happen to me?" he wondered. "Did God have something to do with it?"

After the manager greeted Sinkira again he asked, "You really do want a job?"

"I need work badly. I've been away from my village now for many weeks, but there is little work for someone as young as myself."

"What kind of work can you do? Can I trust you to stay if I give you work?"

"I've been a herd boy, but I can work very hard if you just give me a chance."

The manager wrote his name on a piece of paper, led him to a group of young boys about his age, and showed him the work. Certain weeds grew abundantly on the farm, and the boys were to uproot each of them. They began their work at eight o'clock each morning, and the manager assigned each of the boys a portion to weed. Sinkira thought, "This work is difficult, but I will do my best."

They worked until noon, then went for lunch. After lunch, they reported to the office for the pay for their morning's work. When Sinkira saw each boy receive thirty cents, his eyes grew large. What a lot of money! And when his turn came, they gave him, besides his money, one cup of flour and a liter of milk, because he had no family to feed him.

Each morning when the boys showed up for work and were assigned their portion of the field, Sinkira also was assigned a portion. He worked hard, but he noticed that at times the other boys played around. The manager sometimes whipped them to persuade them to finish their sections. Sinkira just kept steadily working, pulling up all the weeds in his assigned place well before lunchtime, and when the manager began giving him additional areas to clear, he proved capable of doing excellent work.

One day the manager said, "Sinkira, I can see that you are a good worker, so I am going to promote you. You will oversee the other children and see that they keep at their work."

"I appreciate that, Bwana," Sinkira answered.

Sinkira continued as an overseer for about a month. He hid his hard-earned cash in a hole in the floor of the house where he slept. He dared tell no one of his secret hiding place, but each day as he added his few pennies, he thought about what he would do when he had enough money saved.

First, he planned to buy some regular clothes, like the other boys wore. He still wore his dirty sheet, and although he acted as overseer, the boys made fun of his poor clothes when they finished work. Each evening he counted his money, and after one month discovered that he had saved nine shillings. He had never had so much money in all his life and certainly never dreamed of owning that much money.

One day he approached the manager, and asked, "Please, Bwana, may I go into Sotik?"

With the needed permission, Sinkira set out, barefoot and dressed in his dirty sheet. He arrived in the town and purchased a pair of shorts for five shillings and a new sheet for four.

At the end of his second month, Sinkira returned to Sotik and purchased a shirt and a blanket. Now he had everything. How good he felt about himself, his job, and his life. Not once had the manager whipped him. He had proven that the harsh treatment and training received in Masai territorial land served him in good stead for this work. And soon he received another promotion.

He often thought of his mother. Occasionally someone visited that knew about his village, and they brought him news, but that happened much too seldom for Sinkira.

One day he learned that someone trustworthy would be going to Masai territory—to his own village. He opened his secret hole, took out some money, and sent it to Nentayia by this man. In this way he could show her that he still loved her and also that he had work and was well.

Sinkira continued working on the farm for many months. With better food and living conditions, Sinkira grew into a much taller young man, and one day he decided to make a change in his work. He remembered his humiliation at the tea plantation and thought that surely now he stood tall enough to pick tea leaves with the other boys.

"If you go there, you will not get a good salary," one of the boys working with him said.

Sinkira thought about this. He had never asked about a salary at the tea plantation. When he finally went to the manager and said, "I would like to resign," the manager refused to give him permission to leave, saying, "No, you can't leave. You must continue. You work hard, and I don't want you to go."

Although he felt no obligation to this man, he continued working for a while. When a friend from a farm about three miles away heard about his plans to return to the tea plantation, suggested, "If you want to make a change, our farm needs someone just like you. A boy has just been fired, and the job remains open. Are you interested?"

"Just what kind of work is it?"

"You will work only during milking time, feeding the cows."

Accustomed to working hard all his life, this job sounded simple enough. The pay, twelve shillings, appealed to Sinkira, in comparison to the ten he now received, and he left his job of many months and accompanied his friend to the new farm.

Now he had much more spare time, perhaps too much, as he later reflected, but he liked the pay, and he continued saving money to send to his mother.

One day an old friend dropped by for a visit. Among other things, he hinted that things were not going well for Nentayia. Upon closer questioning, Sinkira learned that Nemitil, perhaps in jealousy over the money Sinkira sent to Nentayia, had turned her frustrations toward his mother, not giving her enough to eat or other care needed.

Sinkira went immediately to his new manager and said, "Bwana, I know I have worked only a short time, but I have problems at home and need to go see about my crippled mother."

The manager refused to allow him to leave, even for a few days. Sinkira continued working, but each day brought new worries about his mother. Finally he could bear it no longer and without telling anyone, hurried back to Masai Land, to a village near his home.

He knew that, should he return home, Konoi would surely make good his threat to kill him or to have someone else do it. So he asked friends in this neighboring village to go see how his mother fared and to report to him.

Nentayia sent word back that things were fine with her, she appreciated hearing from him, but the trip was unnecessary.

Sinkira gave his friend thirty-eight shillings, almost all he had left, to take to Nentayia and returned to the farm confident that his job would still be open. His confidence shattered when he heard that the job had already been given to another boy.

"But I have little money and no place to stay," pleaded Sinkira.

The manager reminded him, "I told you not to go. How could I know that you would be coming back?"

"I remember. But I feared for my mother. Now what will I do?"

"You may stay in the home of your friend Leboo here in the labor camp."

"I thank you for being so kind. If you have more work I can do, please let my try again," Sinkira replied.

Sinkira went to stay with Leboo, whose father, a trustworthy man, worked as the watchman. But Leboo became jealous of Sinkira, whom everyone seemed to like.

Sinkira often accompanied Leboo when he went to the property his father guarded. Leboo carefully hid his resentment which built up against Sinkira. Sinkira felt quite at ease with his friend and showed an interest in the farm.

One day when they visited the home of the farm manager, Leboo called, but there was no response. "Good. Let's go in," and he opened the door of the large bungalow.

Sinkira felt uncomfortable going in with no one at home. But Leboo assured him, "Nothing will happen. I do it all the time and no one cares. I want to show you something wonderful." As he crossed the room, he continued, "You know, the manager wants you to stay with us for nothing. Why haven't you gone out to find something to help yourself?"

Sinkira looked at Leboo, speechless.

"Now I want to tell you something. I know where the manager keeps his money," Leboo went on.

Sinkira stopped in his tracks. "I didn't ask to stay with you. I'm hoping another job will open or I would be gone," he said. Then he added, "I don't like to be in this house with no one here."

Leboo had picked up a box and had taken off the cover. "Come. Look at all the money," he urged.

Sinkira crossed the room and stared at the money box. Never had he seen so much money in all his life. "Come. Let's get out of here," Sinkira urged. "We are in grave danger. What if the man returns home?"

Leboo replied, "We can take the money, and you'll be able to have many things for yourself. No one will ever know."

Again Sinkira told him, "Let's get out of here. That would not be a good thing to do." But Leboo took all the money and began dividing it. When he offered Sinkira forty shillings, Sinkira weakened. Leboo kept the remaining twenty for himself.

Sinkira had never done anything dishonest before in his life. He trembled as they left the house. He didn't dare go back to Leboo's place, so he walked to the adjoining farm and spent the night with friends there. He intended to leave the following morning and return to the tea plantation where he had first asked for a job.

His friends at the adjoining farm asked no questions, and he offered no explanation as to his reason for his visit. However, he slept little that night.

Very early in the morning he wakened. He knew the difference between right and wrong. Yet, if he were to return the money now it would get Leboo in trouble. What should he do? His heart felt heavy.

As he sat at the table that morning, he saw his former manager coming and other strange men approaching from the other direction. His heart began to pound. Surely now he was in trouble, deep trouble!

The manager rushed up to him and blurted, "Give back the money right now! Do you still have it?"

"Yes, I have not spent even one shilling," Sinkira admitted.

"Why did you take it? Why did you steal? That's terrible. Now you'll have to go to the police station," the manager said.

The angry manager told Sinkira that his son had been taken to the police headquarters and severely beaten. When Leboo had given Sinkira's name as the one having the rest of the money, the police had released Leboo. "How much of the money did you take?" the manager asked.

Sinkira, ashamed of his part in the theft, answered honestly, "Forty shillings."

He and the manager awaited the arrival of the police. He had betrayed the trust this kind manager had placed in him. He felt sick about it all. Then the police came and began questioning him.

"How come you took the money?" one asked.

Sinkira had been in a lot of trouble before, but never anything like this. "Leboo took me to the house and told me to take some."

"We'll have to take you to the police station with us," they said.

Sinkira anticipated all kinds of terrible things happening to him. However, instead of going directly to the police station, the officers stopped at different homes along the way for a few drinks. As they moved from one home to another, they demanded, "We want *pombe*." No one dared deny them. Soon they had become quite drunk.

While one of the police fumbled for a cigarette, Sinkira pulled out two shillings and gave them to him to buy some cigarettes. In his drunken stupor the policeman mumbled, "Hey, this boy is actually pretty good. I think he did not intend to steal."

Once more the police and Sinkira started to the camp where Leboo lived with his parents. They were all very drunk by this time. They demanded that Leboo give them another twenty shillings.

The boy didn't have the money, since he had already returned the twenty shillings he had kept. His father and mother stood weeping as their son received blow after blow demanding money he had not taken. Suddenly it dawned on Sinkira that the money they had taken would have been the salary of Leboo's father. Now, with no money to help, the parents stood by and watched their son suffer.

A large group gathered to watch the beating, and when one of the men understood the circumstances, he paid twenty shillings of his own money to stop the drunken police. They took the money and left Leboo alone. But before they left one of the policemen turned to Sinkira and said, "We have the money, but we should take you with us to police headquarters anyway."

Sinkira felt fear gnawing at his heart. There was nothing he could do but accompany the police peaceably. The police, knowing the differences between tribes of the Kipsigis and the Masai, realized that if they left Sinkira, a Masai boy, there in a Kipsigis camp after Leboo had been beaten, Sinkira most likely would have been killed before morning, because the Kipsigis would have blamed him for the entire incident.

When they arrived at police headquarters, the policeman to whom Sinkira had given the money for cigarettes invited the lad home with him for the night. He gave him food and a bed to sleep in.

Very early the next morning this policeman made tea for Sinkira and himself, and after they had eaten he asked Sinkira, "Boy, what are you doing so far from home?"

"With no father, the people in my village mistreated me. I feared they would kill me, and so I have been away for a long time," Sinkira explained.

"Never steal, my boy," the kindly policeman said. "It will get you into terrible trouble. Especially because you are a poor boy, stealing will get you into even more trouble. Now I want to help you get out of here. If you stay near this camp until the men arrive for work, maybe some of these men will trouble you, beat you, and mistreat you. They could even kill you. So I want to help you. Now, I will show you the way to get back to your home."

Sinkira knew he could never return home—at least, not yet—but he did know what he would do.

The policeman led him out of the camp, and then he said, "Now, you run for home as fast as you can run. Go well."

"Thank you, and stay well," Sinkira answered and ran as he hadn't run since the elephant had chased him many years before! He ran without looking back, fearful lest someone would be pursuing him. When he was out of breath, he stopped and looked back down the road. He could see no one. He felt relieved. But he also felt a terrible shame for his part in stealing the money. Moving into the bushes at the side of the road, he dropped to his knees and prayed, "Dear God, forgive me for doing such a miserable thing. Help me now as I try to find other work."

After praying, Sinkira felt even more than before that he should return to the tea plantation. At least the young men there, while older, were Masai, and besides, he had grown a great deal since his last embarrassing visit there.

He walked the seven miles to the tea plantation, arriving there in the evening. Several of the young men recognized him. When he asked, "Do you think there is a vacancy now?" they saw that he was much taller and stronger and replied, "We will go check it out at the main office first thing in the morning."

The manager remembered him and agreed that he could try again in the tea fields. The basket now reached only to his waist, and he could pick as many tea leaves as the other young men.

After he worked on the tea plantation about three months, word began circulating among the Masai young men that circumcisiontime would soon be upon them. These older young men belonged to the age group about to be circumcised, and Sinkira listened with interest as they made plans to return to Masai Land for the ceremony. He decided to accompany them and attempt to join the group for circumcision. Surely all past ill feelings would be forgotten when he became a young warrior, or *moran*. Surely if the elders would allow him to join the group of older boys who had already appeared to accept him at the tea plantation, he could live peaceably in Masai Land, go with them to their *manyatta,* and eventully become a warrior in his own right. Then neither Nemitil, Konoi, or any of the other villagers would dare touch him. This could be a chance to prove himself in the eyes of his people and make his mother proud of him. He determined not to say a word of this to the young men until the right time came.

Breaking *Moran* Customs

Sinkira noted with interest the talk among the older boys as they picked tea leaves the next few days. "What day do we need to start our journey back to the village for the circumcision?" one asked.

"About two moons," another responded.

A third reminded them, "The walk is long, so we must be making plans."

They didn't seem to object if Sinkira listened as they made their plans, but they didn't include him, and he made no effort to be accepted.

His work at the tea plantation lasted long enough for him to save ample money to buy his mother some gifts. The night before the older boys planned to begin their long walk back to their Masai village, Sinkira had a plan.

"I want to take my mother some gifts. Do you care if I accompany you back to Masai Land?" he asked.

They saw no reason to deny him, and agreed. So he became bolder and continued, "It would give me great joy if you would accept me in your group for the circumcision. My life at home became unbearable; I've been working these four years. While I am some younger than you, I believe I can be as brave as the rest of you. I want to return to Masai Land."

One of the older boys called the rest together, and Sinkira heard them as they discussed his case. "Do you believe his story?"

"Yes, I have heard of him before and the terrible treatment given him," responded another. "But I don't know if the elders will think he is old enough for circumcision."

"Do we want someone as young as he to be with us, to join our group? In some ways he is like us; at other times he acts very strangely."

"I rather like the boy. Why not let him go with us and see what happens?" And so they agreed to allow him to join their group, and each rolled in his sheet for his last night at the tea plantation.

As pink tinged the clouds the following morning, the young men were up and about. As soon as the manager opened for business, they all resigned their positions as tea-leaf pickers.

"Why didn't you let me know sooner?" the manager asked.

When Sinkira resigned, the manager questioned, "Are you certain that you want to go with these boys? The work here is good, and you are making more money than before."

Sinkira's heart beat like that of a small child as he replied, "I want to go back to my people. It has been much time since I've seen my poor mother."

The manager gave him his papers and asked, "You want to get in on this circumcision too? Aren't you too young?"

Sinkira admitted that his age was below what they usually considered, but he had lived a great deal for his few years, and he did hope to be allowed to join the group.

"Then go well," the manager said.

"Stay well," the boys replied as they began the long walk back to Masai Land.

Little of the conversation involved Sinkira as the boys walked along. Instead of the thin, ill-clad boy of twelve when he left home, he returned a fine, strapping youth of fifteen, proudly carrying a blanket, sheet, some money, and gifts for his mother.

He found that Nentayia still lived with Nemitil and her

husband. The smile she gave her son was enough to make up for the years of trouble now behind him. Sinkira spent some time with his mother. He told her of country rolling away as far as the eye could see, of tea plantations spreading over the hillsides, of the ride on the bicycle, and then on the large tractor. Due to her illness, Nentayia's world had been even more narrow than many Masai. Sinkira watched as she listened with pride, her eyes wide as he told her of these wonderful things. She shook her head when he related the story of the stolen money.

"My son, you are no longer a little boy. You have seen many things and have been many places, and you are a wiser boy. What plans do you have now?"

"I have requested joining the boys who will be circumcised in the next moon," he replied.

"Good. That is good." She spoke with pride, but then Nemitil came in, and seeing Sinkira, began making rude remarks. Nentayia explained his reason for returning, but to Nemitil it made no difference. Sinkira gave her no joy, and she stormed out of the hut in a rage.

Sinkira stayed only long enough for a visit with his mother. When he wondered where he should go until the time of circumcision, Nentayia suggested, "It would be better for you to go live with my brother in his village."

"Stay well, my mother," said Sinkira as he began the twenty-five mile walk to his uncle's village.

The uncle, an orphan and very poor, had a big heart. He and his wife took Sinkira into their home, and he lived there as their own son while the elders decided which of the boys should be circumcised. Each name must be considered individually. They included the age, among other things, and when they came to Sinkira's name, they hesitated. Usually they waited until the young man either reached or neared eighteen. After the customary discussing and debating, they agreed to call Sinkira in to explain why he chose to change his age group and join one older than his own.

He entered hesitantly, and they began questioning him. "Why do you want to change to this group? The things they must do will be hard. Are you certain you are ready for all the difficulties they will be facing?"

Sinkira began, "Many of you know that my father died in battle before I was born. My mother has been ill for many years. I've been working for these four long years. I left home because the villagers treated me badly and threatened to kill me.

Many of the elders, aware of his problems, listened with the others as he continued, "A long time I've been away from Masai Land, and I want to return to my homeland and my people again. This appears the only way I can do that without risking big trouble. If I'm old enough to pick tea leaves, I can be circumcised and prove that I am ready to become an elder."

When Sinkira completed his plea, an elder spoke: "Go now, boy, while we decide with wisdom."

Leaving the hut slowly, Sinkira felt as if many beetles were crawling around in his stomach. Soon the elders notified him that they would allow him to join the group if he could prove capable of all a young man must do to pass the trials ahead.

At last Sinkira felt included. He would be able to do anything, no matter how difficult.

One ceremony remained between himself and circumcision, the ceremony of name-giving. At this ceremony each candidate took a new name—one of his ancestor's names, and added his father's name. The women prepared many drinks, including *pombe*. The men slaughtered a black ox and prepared it for eating while the women cooked other food in readiness for the celebration.

After feasting, all candidates went into one room, and the mothers put tobacco, ground fine rather like snuff, to the young men's noses, ordering them to drink milk as they breathed that *enaisugi*. Sinkira's aunt took the place of his mother, and while the young men breathed the *enaisugi* and drank milk, the mothers named ancestors of the boy's family. As they named these, the boys began sneezing. As priorly instructed, upon sneezing, the boy took the name of the last ancestor named as his new name, after saying "*Tish,*" indicating that he understood and accepted the new name.

Sinkira breathed the *enaisugi,* sneezed, and said, "*Tish.*" He would now have his father's name, Munke, but since he preferred his own name, he became known as Sinkira Munke.

After the name-giving ceremony, every young man's head had to be shaved and his clothing removed. He was dressed in a cow skin especially prepared by removing all hair and smearing it with cow fat to keep the skin soft and pliable.

Meanwhile, the elders sipped *pombe* from a large round pot through bent reeds, waiting for the completion of this rite, which continued through the night. Some of the elders had sons in this group, and they proudly awaited this last ceremony that would make their sons men. Leaving the *pombe* for a short time, the elders went into the room, took ornaments from the mothers, and placed them upon their sons. They reminded the boys, "If you cry out or even move during the ritual in the morning, you will wear these women's ornaments until you die."

Each young man determined that he would not shame either himself or his family. "I'll not have to wear these ornaments ever!" Sinkira vowed.

Soon a group of young men, about Sinkira's age, but younger than the boys to be circumcised, entered the hut and sang to encourage the young men to be brave. Circumcision, the most important occasion in any Masai male's life, required the utmost bravery. Should one even show fear, he would lose his standing in the community forever.

When the singers retired with the grayness that comes before the dawn, the young men threw the skins aside and raced to the nearby stream, where they bathed themselves. Slowly and solemnly they returned to the place of circumcision. Although determined to go through to the end, these young men were strong enough to fight if they changed their minds. Because of this and the possibility of a young man holding a grudge against the one performing the rite, a Masai would seldom perform the procedure. They paid an elder of another tribe, perhaps a Kipsigis.

Upon returning from the river, the boys found the presiding elder seated upon the ground with a skin placed in front of him, and his *panga*, or large knife, in his hand.

Everyone in the village gathered to see which of the young men would be the bravest. To increase their nervousness and to protect the presiding elder, a strong warrior, capable of holding the candidate by force if necessary, stood behind the skin where the young man would sit. Sixteen young men were to participate in this rite of circumcision. As the elder finished with each and the warrior released the young man, the audience cheered, "You are now a warrior," they shouted. "You are brave!"

All the candidates remained in the hut until the last one was circumcised. They huddled against the far wall, eager to retire to the hut prepared for them upon the completion of this ceremony. Then they were allowed to go to the hut, where they remained, hoping the pain would soon pass and they would begin to heal. Each one wrapped the cow's skin, removed before the dash to the river, about himself and tried to get some rest. They could not bathe, but were given a white soil to smear all over the body. Women took them the usual Masai fare. Bleeding meant losing strength, the Masai believed, so extra blood was added to their diet to replace what they lost during the ceremony.

After some time had passed the boys were allowed to leave the hut to hunt for birds of many kinds, which they prepared to be worn around the neck at the ceremony before they went to the bush to further prove themselves. After six months of existing in this manner, the villagers prepared the dismissal feast, and Sinkira with the other young men went to the bush.

Each contributed an ox to take with them. Sinkira, with less than most, managed to add his ox to the others. With some regret he remembered losing his gifts at the cutting of the teeth and the cutting of the ear—yet, he thought now, he wouldn't have done differently could he retrace his steps.

After finding a suitable location in the bush away from the village, they built huts to live in. Each day they went out into the bush to improve their skills as hunters, and occasionally one of them returned to the village to report to the *laibon* in charge, telling him of their progress and asking for guidance and instruction.

On one of the visits the *laibon* sent back bits of powdered charcoal for each of the young men. According to directions, each put his precious portion into a small skin bag worn at all times.

Sinkira watched the others eagerly accepting their portion and thought, "They have small wisdom. Of what value is that charcoal? It is just ashes." When his turn came he refused saying, "This is a trick of the *laibon*. It is only ashes, and I cannot take it."

The other warriors stood aghast! "Does he think he has such great wisdom, greater than our *laibon?*" one asked.

Others began talking more loudly, and Sinkira could hear the anger boiling in them as they openly discussed some of his strange ideas. Finally, the leader said, "If you are against our *laibon,* you should not be in our group."

Sinkira hesitated but a moment. He knew if he left the group he might not be able to go with them to the *manyatta,* but he had been rejected most of his life by villagers. He hoped after a few weeks the young warriors would forget all about this, so he replied, "That is all right with me. I don't like to take this medicine."

The group immediately disfellowshiped him, and before sunup the following morning, Sinkira hurried back to his uncle's hut. Fortunately, the Masai ask few questions, and while he remained there he helped herd cattle, hunted for food, and did other things to bring joy to his uncle's family as he waited for the rest of the young warriors to come out of the bush. He still hoped to go to the *manyatta* with them. He hoped the young men would soon forget the incident that had taken place in the bush. He offered no clue as to his reason for returning. He lived peaceably among the villagers, minding his own business. If they questioned his being there, they held their tongues.

Even though he had left his group, rules that applied to them still applied to him. None of them could open the milk gourd to drink. One of the other warriors always opened and closed the gourd. Now that he lived in his uncle's home, the lid must be lifted by either his aunt or one of the girls. This proved no problem. He called for one of the girls, who brought the gourd, lifted the lid, and passed the gourd to Sinkira, who drank as much as he desired and returned the gourd to the girl, who replaced the lid. Although he had come back from the bush, he resolved to break no more Masai customs, as it would surely end his chance to go to the *manyatta*.

One night he wakened to drunken yelling and laughter, and in the morning learned that during the night the young warriors had returned to the village. With mounting excitement he realized how much he wanted to be with them again. He decided to ask them how things had gone and to see whether they would accept him again into their group.

At the other side of the village Sinkira joined them. When he walked up, they became quiet. He attempted to join in the conversation, asking, "Are you all well?"

Some responded with a grunt; some made no response at all. He tried again, "Are you back in the village to stay?"

Again, a few grunts, but mostly silence, and when it came

time to drink their morning milk, instead of all going in together, they went in by ones and twos, but Sinkira had not been invited in with them. Still, he didn't give up. In a further attempt to make amends, he invited, "You are welcome to my uncle's home."

"I must go herd my cattle and see how well they have done while I have been away," said one. Another replied, "I have important business to complete." Soon Sinkira stood alone.

He returned to his uncle's hut disappointed and lonely. Then anger boiled up inside him. "If they don't want me, I don't need them. I don't need their way of life ever again," he decided and entered his uncle's hut. His uncle's wife brought the milk gourd to him which he had asked her to bring. She placed it in front of him, but when he appeared in no hurry to drink, she left the room.

Sinkira stared at the gourd. He knew the consequences if he continued with his rebellious plans to thwart Masai customs. Slowly he reached for the gourd, lifted the cover, and drank deep draughts of the milk. A strange sensation crept over him, a mixture of frustration, then melting anger, and finally a coming of peace. He stood up and said, "I now have broken one of the *moran's* rules. I will not follow any of them anymore."

He recognized that he had taken a very dangerous step. The older men would think he had little wisdom. The children would make rude remarks about one so stupid. The entire community would look upon him as having green caterpillars inside his head instead of a brain.

Sinkira knew that when the warriors, who had snubbed him that morning, returned to the village and discovered that he had broken another one of their rules he would no doubt receive either a severe beating or even worse punishment. The young men were accomplished in the art of war and of killing. He had good reason to fear them.

But, having broken one of the rules of the *moran,* and

knowing that his aunt would spread the news about his having taken up the gourd, totally against Masai custom, he decided to break another rule. He would wash his hair that had been smeared with rancid cow fat and red soil.

Sinkira took a small piece of soap and hurried to the stream. It took some time to remove all the rancid fat and red soil from his hair. When that had been accomplished, he decided to wash his body sheet, which had also been smeared with the red muddy clay and rancid cow fat. The body sheet reeked of the rancid smell. After washing it, he spread the sheet out on the ground to dry while he sat down to think of some way of escape.

The hot rays of the sun soon dried the sheet, and Sinkira wrapped it around himself and returned to his uncle's hut.

"What have you done?" his uncle cried out when Sinkira entered. "This is a thing of no profit. The young warriors will kill you." His uncle groaned as he spoke.

At first Sinkira had no reply. Then he said slowly, "My uncle, I have found that there is small wisdom and no joy in following the rules of the *moran*. This morning the young warriors rejected me. Now I have decided to go my own way and let them go theirs."

"Oh, but you won't get cows or other animals when you graduate from the *manyatta,* and you will be poor all your life," his uncle reminded him. "Not only that, but I fear for your very life."

"I don't mind. Let us just wait and see what is going to happen when they get back," replied Sinkira. "And I don't mind not getting the gifts. I don't mind any of those things."

When his uncle heard this, he said, "My son, you have given small thought to the warriors when they return. What do you plan to do? What is your decision? You are a young man but no longer a *moran,* so you must have a plan."

"My uncle, I have thought much about this. My plan is to go to school."

"If that is your decision, it is well and good, if you can

find any school where you will be accepted,'' his uncle responded with relief.

Sinkira decided to discuss his decision with his mother and began the long journey to visit her at the first hint of dawn the next morning. He stepped lively as he thought with great happiness of seeing his mother again. The twenty-five miles did not seem long because of his anticipation of seeing her again.

It gave him small joy to find Nemitil at his mother's hut, and when she saw what Sinkira had done to his hair and sheet, she looked at him with scorn. ''You've done some stupid things in your lifetime. You cried when your teeth were cut, so you didn't get any gifts. You refused to have your ears cut, so again, you didn't get any gifts. Now you have rejected the *moran,* and again, you will get no gifts. You are nothing but a stupid boy!'' Nemitil spat out the words and stomped from the hut.

''How is your health, Mother?'' asked Sinkira.

''Good, but my joints still hurt,'' replied Nentayia.

''Listen to my story, my mother.''

''Mm.''

''The *moran* gave me no joy when they returned from the bush to the village. They disfellowshiped me. I no longer choose to become a *moran*. I wish to go to school. I must sell one of my cows to buy a uniform and some books for school.''

''Mm,'' his mother said. Then after a pause she added, ''My son, you have done a dangerous thing. I fear for your life. But I cannot give you permission to sell one of your cows. That is for the villagers to decide.

Just then Nemitil returned and brought half the village with her. ''See, my friends, what my stupid brother has done now.'' She pointed to Sinkira. They looked at Sinkira with disbelief and scorn.

''Why did you wash your hair? Why did you wash your clothes? You always do things without consulting us, and now you have come back to this village for help after you have broken all these rules. Now you will never get any gifts of cows or goats, you will miss many gifts, and moreover the warriors are planning even now to come and beat you for breaking their rules."

Words rushed out of several mouths at once, creating a babel of sound, and Sinkira knew that he could say little more to help his cause. News traveled fast, but still he requested, "Friends, all I ask is that I take one of my cows to sell so I can buy school uniforms and have money for the fees. Is that so much to ask?"

"You were told many years ago that you could never go to school. Surely you are a stubborn-headed boy to hold a desire for so many years," Konoi spoke up.

"Never will we consent to your selling one of your cows for such nonsense," screamed Nemitil.

Other villagers added their dissent, and Sinkira could see that there would be no help from them. They reminded him, "Those warriors will catch you and will kill you."

Sinkira responded, "Don't worry about that."

Konoi finally stated, "No, we cannot allow you to go to school. We told you years ago, but you would not listen to us. Now you come with this decision, this bad decision."

Sinkira stepped over to speak with his mother privately, and she said, "Go in health, my son. I think you have done a good thing, because being a warrior does not benefit anything. Moreover, being a warrior you must do many evil things. Sometimes they steal, and if they get caught they are fined or jailed, and most of the them are killed. I'm happy you have left the *morans*. But I cannot go against your sister and the rest of the villagers, so I cannot let you have your cow. I think you should go to your uncle. I hope he can give you some help."

Tired from the long walk, Sinkira stayed the night, but he felt uneasy in Nemitil's home. He rose early in the morning and whispered, "Stay well, my mother," and she responded, "Go well, my son," as he slipped out into the dawn and started the journey back to his uncle's village.

In spite of his show of bravery, as the sun's rays burst over the horizon, his steps quickened, and he broke into a run. If the warriors were looking for him yesterday, he must not waste any time. He looked over his shoulder many times and darted into brushy places to avoid detection as he hurried on his way. Those warriors were capable of finishing him off completely, and it appeared that the only hope of escaping their wrath was to get accepted into a school as soon as possible, and that took as much money as a cow would bring. How he hoped his uncle could spare a cow!

His uncle showed relief when Sinkira finally dashed through the doorway of the hut and dropped exhausted to the floor. Greeting each other hurriedly, Sinkira began his account of the visit to Nentayia.

"Was your mother well?" inquired his uncle.

"As well as can be expected," responded Sinkira, respectfully. "But Nemitil incited the villagers against me, and she led them in denying me my request to have one of my cows to sell. My mother is asking you to give me a cow so that I may go to a school quickly, as the warriors will kill me for certain if they catch me before I get started in school."

In spite of his uncle's poverty, he gave Sinkira the necessary cow. "Go well, my son," he said. "Take care of the things that need to be done. Be gone as soon as you can, or the warriors may yet catch you."

"Thank you, my uncle. I will try someday to repay you for your kindness to me. Stay well." Sinkira slipped out to the corral, took the cow, and left the village.

Before the light faded he had sold the cow and gone to the nearest school to buy uniforms and enroll. Ironically, the school was located very near his old home village, so he made the journey for the third time in two days, again watching carefully for any signs of the boys who were looking for him, and keeping out of sight as much as possible.

He didn't know what the future held for him, but he knew the past must be put behind, and he must continue forward as he had started. He had gone much too far to ever return to his former ways. As he stood awkwardly at the school door waiting to talk with the headmaster, he wondered, "Is this what God has wanted me to do all the time? Did God tell me what to do?" But he received no answer. His future lay ahead, and he silently asked God once again to help him face whatever might be in store. Somehow Kipkirir's God meant much to him although as yet his knowledge was little.

A Dream Come True

When Sinkira presented himself to the headmaster at the school near Nemitil's home, he experienced mixed emotions. First, the realization that had he not arrived before the *moran* caught him, they would have finished him completely. Second, excitement that, after all these years, he would finally be able to enter school, and last there was the fear that he might not be accepted as a student.

The headmaster opened the door to the tall Masai youth. "What can a young Masai warrior want, coming to school to see me?" he wondered. "What do you want with me?" he asked.

"Have no fear," Sinkira responded, "I only want to go to your school."

"What standard are you prepared to enter?" inquired the schoolmaster.

"Standard? What is this thing, standard? I only want to start in school."

"Do you have the necessary money to begin?" The headmaster hoped this would stop the determined young man.

"I have sold a cow and have money," Sinkira replied.

As they talked, the headmaster sensed that Sinkira truly wanted to go to school. "Why did you wait until now to start school?" he wanted to know.

Again, Sinkira told his story, beginning with his father's death and more recently, of the threat to his life.

The headmaster sensed an honesty and openness in this

young Masai that he admired. The obvious difference in appearance from most Masai young men impressed him, and he filled out the necessary paper work, took Sinkira's money, and walked with him to the Standard 1 classroom. He had failed to warn this proud, tall Masai about what he would find in the classroom, and when he opened the door, the sixteen-year-old boy nearly panicked. After ten years, his dream had become a reality, but he faced children half his age. The highest bench proved much too low for him to sit comfortably.

As the headmaster left, he warned, "Sinkira, you must abide by the rules of this school in order to remain."

Sinkira found his place and looked around. He promised himself that he would learn as fast as possible to avoid the embarrassment of having to sit in class with these little children.

That Monday proved to be an exciting day for Sinkira. As he watched the teacher and listened to him explain the rudiments of Standard 1, he realized how very small his world had been. He saw new horizons opening to him that he had never dreamed possible. This teacher knew just how to show even the smallest child in his classroom how to learn, and although he hardly dared dream just yet, in the recesses of his mind, Sinkira determined that he would learn well and perhaps one day he too could become a teacher.

After school he returned to the home of Nemitil. He didn't expect her to be happy to see him, but he had decided that no matter what it took to go to school, including his sister's mistreating him, nothing could dissuade him. Nentayia secretly told him, "On this very day the young warriors came here looking for you. They were very angry and intended to do you great harm. They asked many questions. When we told them you were in school, they backed out muttering evil things. You can rest easy now. They will not return to hurt you. They fear to do this evil thing."

The *moran* knew the government frowned on the young

warriors spending from three to five of the best and most productive years of their lives cooped up in the *manyatta* instead of doing military service for the country, and they didn't dare interfere with anything having to do with the government, even if it were a parochial school partially funded by the government. Sinkira felt relieved as he realized that he no longer needed to fear them and was free from their clutches.

Sinkira, who stood head and shoulders taller than the other children in Standard 1, often felt foolish when standing with them and especially when reciting, but mid-year another young warrior arrived from a different village, and they became friends. This eased the loneliness and some of the discomfort. Now the two of them wiggled and squirmed, trying to become comfortable on benches intended for small children.

Lepore, his new friend, eagerly learned and proved to be a good student. His brother, a clerk in town, visited occasionally to see how things progressed with Lepore, encouraging him to do his best work. On one visit, he talked a long time with the headmaster. He wanted Lepore to finish Standard 1 and go right into Standard 3, because he appeared to be doing excellent work and was older than most of the students.

The headmaster didn't agree. True, he did excellent work, but he would miss a great deal if he skipped from Standard 1 to Standard 3.

The headmaster talked with the teacher of Standard 1, who agreed that Lepore's grades were among the top, but a few others made equally good grades, he added. To avoid the appearance of playing favorites, the headmaster decided to give all the boys with good grades an opportunity to move on.

Therefore, upon entering the classroom a few mornings later, the headmaster announced, "I wish to see Lepore, Sinkira, and Sankale in the office."

Fear clutched at each heart as the boys left the classroom. Sinkira especially feared for Sankale, his very best friend. Sankale came from a different village, and when he arrived at school, he suffered terribly from scabies. The small children feared him, frightened that they would get scabies too. No one would share a bench with him. Mindful of all the problems he had been through as a young boy, Sinkira had taken pity on Sankale, and although the scabies had been so severe that Sankale's entire body had itched with the dreaded disease, Sinkira had offered to share his bench with Sankale. He had taken him to the dispensary for treatment until the scabies healed, and they had become friends. Now the three young men walked with the headmaster to the office, where he explained that their grades proved that they were capable of doing more difficult work than the younger students. He smiled at the three and said he would now take them to Standard 2 room, where they would be interviewed.

The interview proved to be a test to determine whether the boys, although bright enough in Standard 1, could handle the work of Standard 2. When each passed the test with no problems, the headmaster said, "Now, if you want to move on to Standard 3 next year, you will need to make a change. Instead of coming to school each morning at eight o'clock and staying until noon, you will need to continue in Standard 1 until noon, and then go into Standard 2 in the afternoon."

Sinkira had never considered asking for special favors. While he would willingly have taken each standard as it came, moving ahead would place him in a standard with older students where he could feel more at ease. The three boys thanked the headmaster for his kindness.

Although this made his day much longer, Sinkira didn't complain. Hunger seemed to be with him always. Nemitil refused him breakfast, so he left for school with an empty stomach. With this new program, it meant going without lunch too. But he felt it worthwhile if he could get the education he so desperately wanted. He had waited so long to go to school! He especially enjoyed the classes in Bible study. Finally he could learn of this God who had helped him in so many ways, yet Sinkira felt that he didn't really know Him.

The three friends continued throughout the rest of that school year, studying in Standard 1 in the morning and going into Standard 2 in the afternoon. At the end of the school year, Sinkira realized the Lord had worked another miracle. He had come first in both Standard 1 and Standard 2 classes! Sankale and Lepore also placed among the top six, and all were allowed to pass on to Standard 3 the following year. Sinkira thanked God for this. He had never anticipated doing two standards in one year.

The more Sinkira learned about God from the teachings of this mission church school, the more he wanted to become a part of God's family. Before he finished his first year, he requested baptism. And upon baptism, he took the Christian name of Daniel, retaining his family name, Munke.

Nemitil did all she could to prevent Sinkira from returning to school. She insisted that he herd cattle or do other kinds of work. She refused to give him food in order to discourage his attendance. Many days he had to share a friend's lunch to stave off the terrible pangs of hunger. One of these friends belonged to a different church from most of his classmates. Daniel listened with some interest as they shared lunch. Then one day his friend began telling him about the seventh-day Sabbath, Daniel listened politely but said little. But the more he learned, the more convinced he became that the seventh day was the only day God had sanctified and blessed. He knew that he must begin to obey God on that day.

But now he had a struggle in his heart. If he kept the seventh day holy, how could he participate in his school's races? "I enjoy athletics, especially running. But how can I continue running on the school's competition team, when most of the races occur either on Friday evenings or Saturdays? I now know the seventh day is sacred." He struggled with the idea of giving it up and at last went to the headmaster. He had made his decision. He would keep God's Sabbath day holy.

At first the headmaster became very angry. This young Masai, one of his fastest runners, simply couldn't get by with this! But when he saw Daniel was firm in his decision, he changed his tactics. He planned a long competition tour and showed it to Daniel. While it appealed to him, as he looked it over, Daniel could see that some of the races would be run on Friday evenings or Saturdays. Again he told his superior, "I'm sorry, but I can't run on those days; it would be better if you choose someone who can."

The headmaster, upset not only because of Sinkira's changing from the headmaster's church, but also because of the athletic program he had upset, called Daniel and his Seventh-day Adventist friend to his office again and asked them many questions. Daniel's friend quoted the fourth commandment, and the headmaster listened and then asked, "Won't your church give you dispensation for doing this one thing, running for your school?"

"Sir," Daniel said respectfully, "we are not responsible to the church, but to God."

"If you refuse to run on Saturday, I will expel you from school," the headmaster threatened. It apparently mattered little that Daniel's work in school had been excellent.

Daniel stood before the schoolmaster wondering what would happen next. After all the trouble he had been through, would this be the end of his education? Yet, as Daniel of old, he stood firm and prayed, "God, in Your great wisdom and love, please work it out for me."

"You may have one week to decide whether you will run on your Sabbath or be expelled," said the headmaster before dismissing the boys. "However," he added, "think of all the cities we will be visiting."

"And we would like to go. We would enjoy running for

our school. But we cannot run on our day of rest!" Daniel said firmly.

"But you can rest all the other days and then run only on Saturday," the headmaster begged.

But the boys shook their heads as they answered of one accord, "No, it is not our day but the day of God."

During the week Daniel did some serious thinking. He and his friend, also an excellent athlete, were approached by their friends who tried to change their minds and who begged them to run in the competition for their school.

"You tell me that God has saved your life many times," one friend reminded Daniel. "Now you are in serious trouble. You can even get expelled from school. Where is your God now? Hasn't He forgotten all about you? If you get expelled, maybe you won't even be able to get a job."

When Daniel replied, "It would be of more benefit to me to lose things in this life than to break the commandments of God," his friends turned away, disappointed and disgusted.

At the end of the week, Daniel returned to the headmaster's office. The headmaster said, "Well, Daniel, your friend has decided to be smart and not risk being expelled. He will join our competition. What have you decided?"

"I can't be responsible for anyone but myself. I cannot run on the Sabbath," he responded.

"Get out of this office," the headmaster shouted. "I'll deal with you later!"

As Daniel left the office and started home, he prayed earnestly "God, You know what will happen. You take care of everything for me. I place myself in Your care."

The next morning Daniel went to school as usual, not knowing what reception he would receive. The headmaster met him and invited him into his office. "I have been in contact with each of the other schools competing," the headmaster began, and then looked at Daniel for a long moment. "They have agreed to change the schedule. The running will not be on your Sabbath," the headmaster added.

Daniel looked at the new schedule. Suddenly his heart felt lighter. He couldn't speak.

The headmaster demanded, "Now will you run for us, young man?"

"Yes, that's good. That's good," Daniel agreed. "If the race is going to be on a Friday afternoon and not on the Sabbath, that is no problem at all."

Before the Friday of the competition arrived, Daniel prayed to God for guidance. He realized that there could be more than just this one race at stake. God brought to his mind that should he win in this competition, he would be expected to go on to the district level, and if he should win there, maybe even on to the national. He knew that if he should win, the other competitions would never change their schedules just for one athlete. What should he do?

Like a flash of lightning, he realized that if he did poorly in the final school competition, they would not take him for the competition and would probably kick him right out of the athletic program. Much as he enjoyed athletics, he decided that his only choice would have to be not placing in the competition when they had their next tryouts. He prayed earnestly, "God, I'll do what You want me to do and let You take care of the rest."

The day of the competition arrived. Ideal weather. No recent rains to muddy up the track. No high wind sweeping across the athletic field.

The headmaster blew the starting whistle. One after another the young men began running. Some did well, others poorly. The slower ones were eliminated. When at last the time came for the big race between those chosen to contend in the finals, Daniel lined up with the others. The headmaster gave the signal to start, and all began sprinting to the far end of the field. But Daniel's legs seemed loaded with lead. No matter how hard he pumped them, he couldn't seem to achieve the speed with which he usually ran, and when the race ended, he didn't even place in the competition. In fact, he came in among the very last.

The headmaster looked at him for a long time, not saying anything. Finally he walked over to Daniel and asked, "What happened? The speed you usually have is gone. How could this happen?"

"I don't know what happened," Daniel replied, quite honestly, but puzzled. He knew he should have placed better. He had really tried hard. He had not only let the headmaster down, but the entire school as well. They had even changed the entire schedule with the other schools just for him.

Daniel saw the headmaster walk away from the field, extremely disappointed. For several days he avoided Daniel, but Daniel continued in classes, not knowing from one day to the next what the headmaster would do about him.

The day of reckoning came at last. The headmaster called, "You, Daniel, come here."

Daniel joined the headmaster.

"You are a very good boy in your class," the headmaster said. "I know that you have problems at home. Sometimes you don't get food, and you don't have good living accommodations. Now I want to give you a letter to the government boarding school. There you can get food, you can have a room in which to stay, and you can get help. You can learn even better if your circumstances are improved."

"I appreciate that very much," Daniel responded gratefully.

Immediately the headmaster wrote a letter and gave it to Daniel, who wasted no time in delivering it in person to the headmaster of the government boarding school.

The headmaster of the boarding school accepted Daniel's letter of introduction from the mission school he had been attending. When Daniel went to register, he found that his last name Munke was a common name of many of the students; therefore he decided from then on to be called Daniel Sinkira. At the close of the school year Daniel received his certificate of Primary Education. However, he was not satisfied with having completed Standard 7. He now tried another government school that could make a higher education available to him. But a problem arose. He needed money to attend this school. Where would the money come from? He could depend on no one from his own village nor from his uncle's.

The headmaster recommended that Daniel apply for a loan. However, Daniel discovered that loans were not easy to get. After applying at several places and having been turned down, he decided to apply for work. He could teach in schools up to Standard 7 level. As had become his custom, he prayed for guidance. If he taught for a few years, he could save enough money to go on to higher education.

While attending church services and other meetings at the nearby Seventh-day Adventist church, he saw a young woman whom he admired from afar. Although they didn't date, as that was unheard of in Masai Land, they saw each other in church services and smiled across the congregation shyly. Sinkira asked some discreet questions among the members and learned the girl's name was Leah. "There can't be a more beautiful name in the world!" he thought. Even better, he could see that she belonged to the Masai tribe, and his heart sang, "God is smiling on me!"

Daniel continued attending the church meetings, and the more he watched this young woman, the more he felt drawn to her. He joined social gatherings to be near her and planned, when possible, to attend the same meetings as she. If he couldn't get a loan to continue in school now, then he hoped that she would be willing to wait for him. He didn't dare ask her to marry him when he had nothing to offer her, but her eyes told him that she would be willing to wait. That gave him the necessary incentive to begin looking for work and to continue until he located a job that could improve his station in life. Now he had two goals—to become a teacher and to marry Leah. He must get started and lose no time!

Worth Waiting For

With Leah constantly on his mind, Daniel concentrated on finding a teaching job. He approached the Kenya Office of Education and timidly opened the door. The receptionist referred him to the assistant officer of education.

When Daniel requested an interview with the officer, the man's response neither encouraged nor discouraged him. "Wait outside. I cannot see you now. If you wait, perhaps I can see you later in the day."

Daniel waited. He waited until late in the day and again he quietly knocked on the door. This time the officer told him, "I have no time to see you today. It is time to go home now. Come back tomorrow."

The next morning as Daniel dressed he looked in the mirror and saw his tattered clothes. "Ah," he said, "I am indeed poor, but I am clean." And he sent up a prayer to his heavenly Father as he left for the Office of Education.

To his question, "Now may I have an interview?" the officer gave him more excuses, and after waiting the entire day, Daniel returned to his room, discouraged.

The day following he went again to the office. Again he waited all day to no avail. Each day placed him at the office door, but each day another excuse prevented him from the interview that he requested. The assistant appeared a very busy man, coming and going, but he never had time to spend with the patient Masai who waited outside his door.

Daniel prayed each day for guidance and help. If he could

only talk with the officer, he felt sure he could persuade him to at least give him a chance to prove whether or not he could teach. Friday morning Daniel again returned to wait outside the door. When the officer left the office that morning, he promised, "I will talk with you when I return."

Daniel waited, and as he waited, he prayed, "Lord, You know that tomorrow is Your Sabbath. Please help me to get the interview today."

The officer returned late in the afternoon and said, "I'm sorry. But you can come again tomorrow."

Daniel felt defeated. He could never apply for a job on the Sabbath, but before he spoke, the officer's driver spoke to the officer: "Why do you keep this young man waiting? Why don't you tell him something? Why don't you tell him there is no work here, so he can go someplace else? Why are you keeping him here for nothing? Why not just tell him to go away and not bother you anymore?"

The officer shrugged his shoulders. Suddenly he turned to Daniel and invited him to step into his office. He thanked him for being so gracious and for waiting so patiently, then abruptly he asked, "You say you want to become a teacher? What are you going to teach?"

Daniel had given that very little thought, assuming the officer would tell him what to teach if he gave him a job, but he responded, "Whatever the other teachers are teaching."

"And just what are they teaching?"

Daniel prayed for guidance. His answer, he knew, would be crucial in whether or not he got the job. After thinking for a moment, he replied, "The other teachers are teaching the syllabus of Kenya. That is what I will teach."

To Daniel's amazement and joy the officer said, "Good. Now I am going to give you a job. I want to thank you for your brief answer. You answered the way you should."

The officer wrote a letter and gave it to Daniel, told him he would be teaching in a government school in Osinoni, about seven miles from Kilgoris Town.

Daniel, somewhat stunned by the interview, thanked the man profusely. He left the office, bewildered, thrilled, and perhaps most of all, terrified of what lay ahead. He wondered whether all teachers felt the same way before they faced their first school.

Returning to his room at the boarding school, Daniel wearily fell into bed and slept. He felt certain that God intended that he have this job, and if God intended that he have it, God would be with him as he began the largest undertaking of his life. Sabbath morning he shared his experiences with those at church and made certain that Leah knew he had work. His friends rejoiced with him and wished him well.

The following Monday Daniel went down to the school at Osinoni. The headmaster took one look at Daniel, a boy he had known many years before. This boy was now being sent to him as a teacher! Daniel had not attended the bush schools, and the headmaster reminded him of this now. "What have you done that you deserve this letter from such a good school? When you were in the bush you didn't attend school."

Daniel remembered his longing to attend school and of the circumstances that had made it impossible for him at that time. He remembered the struggle he had had to get through the seven standards he had now completed, but he replied "Yes, I have now attended school and have completed Standard 7." He would not mention the past.

"May I see the school syllabus?" Daniel asked. Of course, he really did not know if a syllabus existed in writing or not.

Imagine his relief when the headmaster gave Daniel the syllabus! He also showed Daniel other books and material available to teachers for use in the classroom. Daniel breathed a prayer of thanks and elation as he started home with the syllabus.

Daniel learned that he would be teaching with another more-experienced teacher. Usually there were three teachers at the school, but Daniel learned that the two of them would do the work usually done by three. Fortunately he was not afraid of work and determined to do his very best.

Daniel showed up at school barefooted and wearing his ragged shorts. He could do no better. However, he was always clean. The students learned from him quickly and loved him for his Christian understanding and concern. After three weeks, the other teacher loaned him money to buy a pair of shoes and some long trousers.

Soon everyone in Osinoni loved Daniel. Although Daniel was teaching in a small village school, everyone soon knew him to be a Seventh-day Adventist Christian by the way he conducted himself, both in the classroom and out.

At the time of the school break he hurried back to the school where his beloved Leah waited for him. Until this time, they had never talked alone together. Now he requested a personal talk with her and asked her to become his wife. Without hesitation she replied Yes, and Daniel's heart felt it would burst with pride and happiness.

During different times of visiting in groups, Daniel had told Leah of his many childhood abuses, about his problems, his aspirations, and most of all, about his mother. Leah asked him to take her to his mother's village to meet his family and fellow villagers.

Nentayia and Leah loved each other at first sight. Even Grandmother approved of Daniel's choice of a bride. And this was strange because usually a Masai father chose a son's wife. In Daniel's case, it should have been some other relative, probably his uncle with whom he had lived for some time. Choosing his own wife and taking her to meet Nentayia meant breaking yet another Masai cultural rule.

Daniel and Leah, who were Christians, no longer feared the consequences of breaking with old customs. Following the visit in Daniel's home village, he and Leah were married in a quiet ceremony on February, 18, 1970, at the Oloiborsoito Seventh-day Adventist Church. The church members witnessed the wedding, performed by Pastor Hezion Kinani, the Field President of the South Kenya Field at that time.

Non-Christians refused to attend the wedding. They considered the Christian wedding to be wrong—not performed according to Masai custom. They accused Daniel and Leah of being slaves to western culture. Although performed in a church, the ceremony had some similarities to Masai culture. The pastor blessed the bride and anointed her head with butter before the closing prayer. She received instruction concerning how to live peacefully with her husband, even in times of trouble, and how to care for her future family. But at the reception the usual *pombe* and flesh food were not served, nor were any of the heathen rites performed.

At twenty-two, Daniel felt that he had almost everything he could want. He made more money than ever before in his life. He had repaid the loan for his first school clothes, and he owed no man. He loved his wife, and she loved and cared for him and their home. He enjoyed his teaching career, and they had all the necessities of life and some to spare. However, Daniel had a burden for his crippled mother. Nemitil and her husband still cared for her, but Nemitil's husband wasn't well, and Nemitil turned to *pombe* more often as the burdens became heavier. She had five children, the youngest only two years old.

Soon after Daniel and Leah were married, Daniel's grandmother, although still a pagan, came to live with them. Her feelings had long since changed toward him, and Daniel and Leah cheerfully accepted her into their home.

Kamagambo

Daniel put all of his time and energy into his teaching. Meanwhile, his church responsibilities increased. With Leah beside him, living became a sweet, happy experience for the first time he could remember. Everything seemed to be moving along, and his future appeared settled until he met J. N. Kyale, principal of the Kamagambo Teacher's Training School. Principal Kyale came to the village where Daniel taught. As they visited, he mentioned the possibility of Daniel's attending Kamagambo to further his education.

Daniel remembered that students from the school had conducted a few meetings in his village when he was a herd boy. Villagers had refused his request to attend the meetings, and he had reluctantly put his desires to rest. Now some of the students were working among the people of Osinoni. The meeting of the principal of the school and Daniel, proved to be another turning point in his life.

"Why don't you make a trip to Kamagambo at the end of your term to take an entrance examination?" the principal asked Daniel.

Daniel hesitated, then replied, "I must talk first with my wife, and then we will pray about it."

The idea excited him, but attending Kamagambo would also cost money. Where would the money come from? Finally he blurted to his wife, "Leah, Principal Kyale wants me to go to Kamagambo for a test. If I pass, I can be accepted there as a student and learn how to be a better teacher."

"Then perhaps you should go," Leah said with a smile.

"But Kamagambo costs money. How will we pay the tuition if I do become accepted?" Daniel asked.

"Of that matter I have small wisdom, but we shall pray to our God. If He wants you to go, He will prepare the way." And they knelt in prayer for guidance.

The impression that he should go became stronger even as they prayed, and when they finished, neither had any doubt. Daniel told Principal Kyale he would go, if the testing could be on a day he was free.

When the principal returned to Kamagambo, he talked with some of the faculty. They agreed to give Daniel the necessary test on a Sunday and sent word to him of the date.

Daniel and Leah now had no doubts. Daniel should enroll in school at Kamagambo. Daniel rose early on Sunday morning and hailed a *matatu*, or pickup, with benches in the covered bed, paid his fare for the ride, and began the fifty-mile ride over rutted roads to the training school. The *matatu* careened around corners, sliding from side to side on the muddy road. At Kisii he transferred to another *matatu*.

At last he saw the sign, "Kamagambo Secondary School." He signaled the driver, and the overloaded vehicle jolted to a stop, then lurched on its way almost before he jumped down. The driveway leading to the green campus looked inviting, and he walked to the administration building, where he made arrangements. Carefully, prayerfully, he answered all the questions and returned the test sheet to the teacher asking, "When can I expect to have an answer?"

To his surprise and delight, the teacher replied, "If you can wait, you may have your answer today."

As Daniel waited, many things flashed through his mind. "If you ever ask to go to school again, I will finish you off completely!" How long ago that seemed, yet he still remembered the hurt and also his resolution that one day he would go to school.

"No, we cannot allow you to sell one of your cows. We told you long ago. You are a stubborn, stupid boy!" Those words had also hurt him deeply, yet he had found a way. God had honored his heart cry, and while in school he had become one of God's children.

"Daniel."

The voice interrupted his reminiscing, and he sprang to his feet. "Yes?"

"Here is your test. You may take it to Principal Kyale's office before you return to Osinoni."

Daniel stared at the results in disbelief and hurried to the office indicated. He handed the papers to Principal Kyale, who looked at the grades and invited Daniel to have a seat.

"Daniel, these grades indicate that you may be accepted here next school term. Do you wish to attend Kamagambo?"

"Yes, sir, I would like to come here. But many things must be decided. I have a teaching job now, and I have a wife. May she also come? And is there some work that I can do to pay for the tuition?"

The principal shook his head. "We're sorry, Daniel, but we have no place for husbands and wives. We have only rooms for students. Your wife would have to remain in the village. But we do have some work. Go home, talk it over with your wife, and pray about it. We will mail the official acceptance, and you can let us know what your decision is after you have received it."

Daniel returned home elated yet sad. When he told Leah the results of his test, he added, "But they have no room for wives. I don't like to leave you here in the village."

"God has made it possible for you to go. He will take care of me and show us the way," Leah answered.

Daniel remained at home the rest of the week, eagerly waiting for the official acceptance to arrive by mail. His mind wandered from his teaching as he began making plans for Leah to return to his home village while he would be away. Both felt it wiser for her to go than remain in Osinoni.

The treasured acceptance finally arrived. The new term started soon, and when Daniel went to the office of education with his resignation, the officer begged, "Please stay on with us. You are better than most of our teachers."

"That's because I'm a Christian. I don't drink *pombe* or waste time on ceremonies," Daniel thought. He explained his reasons for wanting to return to school and finally promised, "When I complete my two years at Kamagambo, I will return and teach for you."

Daniel had taught school for one year as an untrained, unqualified teacher, yet his record stood for itself. He knew that he had employment waiting when he completed his studies, and he returned home to begin packing. As he packed, he realized that his year of teaching prepared him for continuing his education. Not only could he now afford to go to a school for further education, but he knew that with more training he could become an even better teacher. In the year he had taught at Osinoni, he had earned a good salary. Instead of the one pair of worn shorts, he now owned several pair of long trousers, shirts, plus many other things. On top of everything, he placed his most valuable possession, his Bible.

He helped Leah and his grandmother get their household items together, carried them to the roadside, and waited with them for the *matatu*. They shoved their household items under benches of the *matatu* when it arrived, loaded some on top, and attempted to hold the balance in their laps for the few miles to his home village.

The villagers welcomed them, and they settled into an old hut near Nemitil and her family. It pleased Grandmother to be back. At first the villagers accepted Leah, but soon they considered her to be an outsider. Daniel could sense this. How he hated to leave her.

The day arrived when Daniel loaded his box of personal items on a *matatu* and barely jumped in before it continued its breakneck speed toward Kisii. He finally arrived at Kamagambo. As he walked beneath the spreading branches of the trees lining the road that led to the campus headquarters, he felt at peace with God and the entire world. It seemed at long last he had come home.

Daniel studied diligently and entered into school activities. He enjoyed the Christian fellowship that warmed his heart. But he missed Leah. So many things happened that he longed to share them with her, especially when, at the end of the first year, he was ordained as a deacon. Such happiness should be shared, but it cost several shillings to go home. And he had all too few—just enough for him to stay in school. But he visited home some week-ends and during the vacation time each three months. Then he tried to remember the many happy times and share them with Leah and encourage her.

She also had things to share with him, and some of the stories she related to him proved beyond any doubt that God continued to care for them and lead in their lives.

One Masai custom, especially, made life difficult for her. When the young men were in the *manyatta,* they often went to the bush for a prearranged visit with women from the village, often other men's wives. They would become lovers and meet repeatedly. The women encouraged Leah to go with them to meet these *moran*. When she refused to go, she heard some say, "She has no wisdom in her head. She has no enjoyment in life."

While they didn't speak of it publicly, the Masai accepted this as a part of their customs. This woman Daniel married appeared to them every bit as strange as Daniel, and Daniel had been different most of his life by refusing the Masai ceremonies and life-style. As they had rejected Daniel, they now rejected his wife and made life miserable for her. Leah longed to be accepted and have friends, but the love of God and of her husband kept her from doing things Christians could not do. As Leah related these things to Daniel, it reminded him of the hatred the villagers had once shown him. It also concerned him for her safety and made him all the more lonely for her when he returned to school.

After one separation of several weeks, Leah had something special to share with Daniel when he visited—they were going to have their first child. Daniel didn't think anyone could be happier and more proud than he, yet his concern deepened. Now that Leah carried their first child, he knew the villagers would attempt to force their heathen customs on her. She broke tradition by eating things normally forbidden by the Masai for pregnant women. She drank milk and did not inquire about its source. Masai custom forbade a pregnant woman to drink milk from a deformed cow. The villagers taunted her and truly believed her child would not be normal. She also refused to wear stick charms around her neck to protect her unborn child from deformity. Daniel's sister, Nemitil, still cared for Nentayia, as well as for her ailing husband, but she had time enough to let Leah know how she felt about the broken Masai customs and traditions. It appeared that the hatred Nemitil felt for Daniel now was transferred to his wife.

When the village women gave her an especially hard time, Leah reminded them, "As a Christian, I depend upon my God. He will take care of me and the child I'm going to bear." But both she and Daniel knew that if she bore an abnormal child, the villagers would blame not only Leah, but Daniel and their God as well.

During one of his holidays, Daniel decided the time had come to repair their hut, which was made of poles and grass. This hut had stood for many years with no repairs, and after studying the many needs, they decided it would be wiser to build a new one. The responsibility of preparing the grass for the roof belonged to the women. But Daniel felt that since Leah was pregnant, she shouldn't do such heavy work, so he joined her in cutting the grass. He also cut the poles for her.

The villagers watched him doing woman's work in amazement and disgust. Daniel must have taken leave of his senses! No man ever helped his wife with such a thing. Masai custom forbade it. Some of the villagers asked Daniel, "Why are you cutting grass with your wife? This is not an act for a man to do."

Daniel replied, "She is my helpmate, she is my body, she is a part of my body, so we should share things together. I should help my wife if I can."

The villagers began abusing Daniel, using evil words, calling him stupid, and threatening with even worse dealings. Daniel didn't care for himself, but he did feel fear for Leah and dreaded leaving her alone again. Even though his grandmother still lived with Leah, she now had no sympathy for their strange ways and offered no help to Leah.

When Daniel next returned home, he found that Leah had been the brunt of the villager's taunting and abuse since he had last visited. She began to feel that perhaps her life could be in danger. She told Daniel, "Even our relatives are very critical of what we are doing. Our lives are going to be in a very critical situation. These people may be stupid, but they can also inflict a great deal of harm to us."

They spent much time in prayer together. Daniel encouraged Leah with the words: "This is our chance to witness what Christian living is all about—what being a Christian really means. We can show them that Christians live together, stay together cooperatively, helping each other. This is the time to show how Christian families live." Daniel and Leah continued to set a Christian example before the village people, who soon began comparing their lives with the Christians.

Knowing of the high mortality rate of Masai children, Daniel planned for Leah to go to a hospital for their first child. Again, village tongues wagged. "Unheard of. What is the man thinking about? Aren't our midwives good enough for him and his wife?'' And they anticipated all kinds of abnormalities because of the broken customs and traditions.

Daniel was away at school when Leah realized that her baby would soon arrive. While she didn't relish the rough ride, she managed to squeeze into the already over-crowded *matatu* and traveled the five miles to the Kilgoris Hospital. On August 31, 1972, she gave birth to a perfect baby boy. Both she and Daniel were jubilant and thanked God that once again He had helped them witness for Him. They named their firstborn Meshack and proudy took him home, where the villagers all examined him, expecting the worst. They looked at his eyes; they felt his legs. They rubbed his head. They searched over his tiny body and found no defects or abnormalities. One at a time the villagers left the hut quietly, most of them ashamed of their former conduct and criticism of Leah. Recently a midwife had delivered a deformed baby, in spite of the mother's keeping all the Masai traditions, and some of them began to soften in their attitude toward Leah. To bear a perfect firstborn, a boy! They shook their heads in disbelief.

Leah watched as Meshak grew day by day and month by month. He was fair, he was good, he was strong and healthy. What more could a mother want? And her faith in God also increased from day to day, even though life in the village still remained difficult. With the baby doing well, some of the villagers tried new ways of taunting Leah, ''Why do you let that lazy husband of yours continue going to school? While he taught you had much money. Now you have no money at all. Why don't you get him to teach again so that you can have lots of money like you did before?''

Leah, well aware of their financial problems, continued to live the best she could, looking forward to each visit from Daniel. She didn't complain, for she knew that each visit home meant that it was much closer to the time when he would finish at Kamagambo and they could once again live as they had when he had taught at Osinoni, perhaps even better. Money meant little to Leah, but food—all the food they needed sounded good.

At the end of his second year at Kamagambo, Daniel graduated with honors. True to his word, he contacted the Government Education Office. They welcomed him and gave him a school in Masurura. Waiting for his family to join him, Daniel stayed in the home with another teacher's family, and while there had good reason to remember the village customs, especially concerning the *laibon*.

After retiring one night he heard a group approach the house singing the praises of the *laibon*. He recognized that they were a group called the "chosen nine" who accompanied the *laibon* from place to place, either to bless or curse, as the occasion demanded. Most of these people were Catholic, yet they continued with their ancient customs. The singers neared the house, stopped, and then entered. Daniel listened as the *laibon* conveyed a prophecy of things to come. His intent was obvious. He brought a message to that house, expecting good pay for his services.

"Don't make so much noise!" the lady of the house cautioned. "What's wrong?" they asked.

"Well, the new teacher is in bed, and he's tired and resting," she replied.

The *laibon* stopped and questioned, "Who's that?"

"Daniel Sinkira," she replied.

Daniel knew that he was well known by this *laibon*. He heard him tell the chosen nine, "Don't praise me anymore." He started to sing a Christian song.

Then the *laibon* stopped singing and said, "I want Daniel to come here."

Daniel dressed quickly and went to greet the *laibon*.

"My friend," the *laibon* began, "I want you to baptize me."

Daniel knew the *laibon* feared Christians. Now he claimed he wanted to become one of them, but deep in his heart he was still a *laibon,* and until he could accept Jesus as his Saviour and give up his ways, he could not become a Christian. Daniel explained all this. "Are you certain that you want to leave all these things for Jesus and be baptized?"

The *laibon*, much as the rich young ruler had done, turned away. He left the house with his chosen nine, a great deal quieter than when he had entered.

Soon Leah and Meshack joined Daniel at Masurura. Teaching became his life again. He enjoyed time spent with his wife and son. Soon they had enough money to buy necessary items, and before the school year ended, a few luxuries graced their home. Grandmother also made the journey to join them, and the following year the government moved them to teach in a school in Ramosha. On April 22, 1976, a baby girl was born to Leah and Daniel. Leah once more went to the Kilgoris Hospital for her delivery. They named the baby Naomi, "My Delight." First a son and now a daughter—and both perfectly healthy! The people at Ramosha marveled at her perfection, knowing that her parents no longer held with their former traditions.

During this school year, Nemitil put her husband into the government hospital, where he could get professional relief from his terminal cancer. Daniel visited him, remembering his kindnesses when all the other villagers treated him so badly as a boy. He shared in the mourning when he passed away. Nemitil listened to Daniel when he suggested that she bury her husband in the government cemetery, so they held a quiet graveside service. When the villagers returned home, they killed a fat ram, stripped off the fat, and heated it to boiling. After it became liquid, they annointed his ornaments, then roasted the flesh and ate it.

Relatives and children shared in receiving the annointed ornaments. Nemitil grieved the loss of her husband, but she didn't suffer hardships as in old times. A new age had come. Widows now were not shunned as they once were. A widow was now free to do as she pleased. Unfortunately, Nemitil turned even more to drinking of the ever-present *pombe*. She seemed unable to face reality.

Daniel continued teaching in government schools. And a few months after Nemitil lost her husband, he moved his mother to his home. Even with the increase of family size, Daniel made good money, and they had need of nothing. His reputation as an outstanding teacher grew, one the government valued highly. He taught four years for the government, and the officials felt that Daniel's future with them would be a good one, both for Daniel and for their school system.

During his fourth year of teaching, the pastor involved Daniel in church responsibilities unfamiliar to him. He could teach children, but could he teach adults? He would try, with God's help, to do his best. Until now he had felt his life complete and lacking in nothing, but a question began to plague him: "Am I doing what the Lord wants me to do with my life?" Daniel began to pray earnestly that God would guide him.

All the Way With Jesus

Each month Daniel made a trip to Kisii to collect his salary. Usually he returned the same day, but one time he stayed two days to care for some business and visit with friends.

Leah remained behind at Masurura with the children. Upon his return, friends rushed to meet Sinkira, telling wild tales of terrible things that had happened to Leah in his absence. Daniel hurried home, where he found Leah completely distraught. Bit by bit he managed to get her to tell him what had happened.

Two village women pretended friendship with Leah and invited her to go with them to gather firewood the day Daniel had stayed in Kisii. They knew that Leah was a Christian. But they planned to have her meet some Masai warriors. They themselves thought the customs of the Masai were better than that of Christians. When they reached a prearranged place, they found three warriors waiting for them, and two of the men immediately began to assault the other two women, who were willing to co-operate.

Leah, horrified by what she was witnessing, said, "No. We're Christians, and we don't do that. It is against the commandments of God, and that is a sin. You are doing something very, very bad before God." She tried to avoid the warriors.

Fully expecting her to comply with his wishes, the warrior asked, "What are you? Why are you complaining?

Your husband is gone. The other two women have accepted. Do you think you are different from the other women?"

She tried to explain that her being a Christian made her different. The warrior became very angry and tried to take her by force, but Leah saw that the warrior was much taller than she was and much stronger. She held in her hand a *panga,* a long knifelike tool used in cutting wood. Her only chance to escape was to stop him by force, so she bent down and swung her *panga* against the warrior's leg with all the force she could muster.

The warrior went down, his leg broken and bleeding badly, and Leah ran from the scene. When the other warriors saw what she had done, they gave chase and began throwing their *orinkas,* or clubs with steel ends, and one of them struck her in the back. She fell to the ground. But she sprang up and ran all the way to the police station with her clothes torn and her arms and legs bleeding from the thorn bushes that clutched at her as she fled.

The police listened as she told her story. They could see how badly she was hurt. They gave her a letter that would protect her for a while, stating that she had also been injured. The wounded warrior was taken to the hospital.

Daniel took Leah in his arms and tried to comfort her, but they both knew that they could be in for some difficult days ahead. Never before had a Masai warrior's advances to a woman been refused. Surely the Masai would not accept this.

Some of the village elders felt that, at the very least, Leah should be heavily fined. Others thought she should be killed. Daniel and Leah prayed most earnestly during this time, and some of the wiser elders suggested, "Let's have a meeting first, to see what she has to say. If we are defeated, this case can go to the government."

They called the meeting and invited Daniel to meet with them. "Your wife cut the warrior, and this thing has never been done before," they reminded him. Couldn't she just have walked away? She cut the warrior, but the other women consented to the men. Why did she have to cut the warrior?"

Daniel explained, "You see, we are Seventh-day Adventist Christians. We are a different kind of people. Our women are only for us. We don't commit adultery as other men do. Adultery is a sin."

"Yes, we think this teacher is right," some admitted. But some of the other elders disagreed. "No. It is against our customs. She must be punished."

Leah showed the letter from the police to Daniel. "Should I not use this letter?" she asked. "It will condemn the warriors that tried to assault me."

But Daniel suggested, "Let us just wait and see what they are going to do about it. I don't want to use the letter unless it is necessary."

The injured warrior's father wanted justice for his son, but when he tried to bring more trouble, Daniel at last showed him the letter, and the father changed his mind quickly. "Oh, these people are different, and they are right for not committing adultery," he said and dropped the case against Daniel and Leah.

"When I recover, I will kill this woman. I will hunt her down until I finish her off completely," the wounded warrior vowed.

"It may be safer for you to leave the village," some warned Daniel and Leah.

"Maybe you should teach in a different school," they told Daniel. But faith in God sustained them, and the warrior left them alone, making trouble for someone else.

Over his years as a Seventh-day Adventist, Daniel had held the offices of chorister, Missionary Volunteer leader, Sabbath School superintendent, and deacon. He took his deacon's work very seriously, doing such an excellent job that the church ordained him as elder. During his fourth year at the Ramosha School the district pastor leaned heavily on Daniel's support. Many members had become upset over differences among themselves and had scattered.

The district pastor, already overburdened, asked Daniel, as an influential layman and elder, for assistance in bringing the congregation together again. Daniel knew these people well and understood many of their problems. He realized that it would take much time usually spent preparing lessons, yet he humbly accepted the challenge, worked with the people, and with the Lord's help, succeeded in bringing most of the discouraged members back to the church.

God had truly been good to Daniel and his family. Yet, as he worked with the people of the church, assisting the pastor in helping many return, he began to feel a seed of discontent stir within him. He couldn't understand it. He enjoyed his teaching, he loved his family, and eagerly looked forward to the birth of another child. Yet, when he worked with the wandering members of the church and felt the satisfaction of seeing a lost one return, the discontent increased. A thought continually nagged in the back of his mind—was he doing all he could for the Lord he loved so much and who had been so good to him?

At first he couldn't speak of it to Leah. Toward the end of the school year he began teaching Bible classes in his home for interested village people. A few began attending, and then more and more. Leah watched and listened as he taught the people about the God whom they both loved. Finally he confessed to Leah about the burden on his heart to help win more people to Jesus, to become a full-time worker for Him, and Leah, having seen his success, surprised him with her encouragement.

Masai measure their wealth by the number of cattle owned. While Daniel had no cattle, he made better money than before, since receiving the teaching certificate from Kamagambo. Some Masai envied the material things he could afford. Yet in his heart Daniel felt the Lord calling him, so with mixed feelings he carefully worded his resignation from teaching one evening. He knew that from then on their lives would be totally different. Their living standards would have to change, and that with two small children and soon a third, life wouldn't be as easy as it had been the past four years.

When he presented his resignation to the headmaster, the man sat speechless at first. Then words tumbled out, "You are my best teacher. I can trust you, and you are making good money, yet you say you want to go to work for some church! I must take this to the board, but I know that they won't want to accept this foolish thing you are doing."

A few days later he called Daniel in again, and this time some higher officials were with him. They also tried to dissuade him by offering him more money if he would stay on with them. When he continued to refuse, they suggested that he take a few days to think about it and let them know later.

Daniel returned to the classroom and finished out the day, then hurried home to discuss everything with Leah. The promotion and larger salary tempted him at first, but as they talked, Leah encouraged him to follow through with what he felt the Lord wanted him to do.

When he returned to school the following morning he notified the headmaster that he appreciated all their confidence in him, but he felt he must follow where the Lord led. The headmaster accepted with regrets the resignation, wondering where he could find another teacher, a nondrinker, trustworthy, and qualified.

Word soon spread among the villagers that Daniel Sinkira would not teach the next school year. "How stupid you are," some told him. "Think of the money you'll be giving up," said another. "Before you began teaching you were very poor. You had no shoes, no trousers, nothing but a sheet. Now you have a family, and you will soon be poor again. Do you think that these people you are going to work with will support you? They are crazy. You are crazy for wanting to preach for them. You will be poor the rest of your life."

Daniel listened patiently to all their arguments. "Look," he said, "if I resign from this work, then I will be doing the work of my God for the rest of my life. I am the son of a living King, a king who is the King of kings, and He will supply all my needs. All that I need in this life and in the life to come, He will supply."

He didn't expect them to understand. Nemitil and other relatives tried to discourage him. They complained, "You are looking for a downfall. Your family is growing up. You remember the difficulties you had before, and now you are going back to the same kind of thing again. Do you expect that mission to support you?"

"I do not depend upon Christians or on the mission. I depend upon God." Daniel spoke confidently. And when they continued to accuse him of being cheated by crazy people, he didn't waver in his decision.

Before he left the school at the end of the term, government officials went to him and reasoned, "You want to be a minister, but in case you should change your mind, may we leave your name on our books as a teacher for five years? We will give you a leave of absence of five years, because you have been a good teacher. You are one of the best we have. You don't drink *pombe*. We are pleased with your work, and we don't want to lose you."

Daniel responded, "I appreciate your kind words and thoughts, but I'm not afraid of the way I'm going. I have no doubts. I don't want to remain a teacher. I want to be a minister," and he left the government officials speechless.

At the end of the term, in January of 1977, Daniel left the school where he had so many fond memories and joined the ministerial students in the South Kenya Field. He was assigned to the Kilgoris district, with six churches to pastor. He worked quietly among the people there, and while the pay didn't come up to a government teacher's salary, he and Leah found that the Lord helped them stretch what they had to take care of their needs.

Leah remarked one day, "You know, when we had so much money, we always spent it all before the end of the month. Now we don't have as much, but it lasts until the month is gone, because we don't buy foolish things with it as we did before."

In July of 1978 God blessed Daniel and Leah with another little girl, Norah. Daniel's old grandmother still helped with things around the house. While neither she nor Nentayia, his mother, accepted Christianity, both respected Daniel and Leah for what they believed and the way they lived.

It seemed now that Nentayia grew weaker each day. In spite of her crippling disease, she had outlived many of the other villagers. In November 1978 she passed to her rest.

Daniel arranged a quiet Christian funeral for her, a song, a verse of Scripture, and prayer. He regretted that although she understood Christianity, she had not accepted it.

Daniel did a good work in the South Kenya Field. He enjoyed his work, but he realized that to be more effective, he needed to return to Kamagambo and take their preliminary ministerial course. It meant more months of separation, but again Leah agreed that it must be, although they now had three small children.

Daniel requested admittance to Kamagambo, and they welcomed him back. His former scholastic record stood on its own merit. The conference kept Daniel on its payroll while he attended Kamagambo, studying the Bible, the best syllabus in the world. He would study for three months, then return to his home and work with his people for three months.

In March 1981 workers from Kamagambo drove to the village and took Leah to witness Daniel's graduation from the preliminary ministerial course. Recent heavy rains left the roads muddy, but the slipping and sliding of the car didn't mar her pride or joy. When they drove onto the campus, Leah marveled at the beauty and beamed with pride as Daniel received his diploma, especially knowing that he finished at the head of his class.

At thirty-three years of age and with a family of four small children, little Jane having joined the family during Daniel's last year at Kamagambo, the conference assigned Daniel to a new pastorate, living in Narok and having two other churches to shepherd.

The move to Narok proved more complicated than any before. The distance was great for his elderly grandmother. It seemed unwise to move her. She was almost a hundred years old. Daniel and Leah helped her settle in with Nemitil to help Nemitil with her chores and guide the teenage daughter who remained at home.

Little had been done for the Masai in the Narok area prior to this. Still resistant to change, they are a difficult people to reach. But Daniel, on his trusty motorcycle, traveled the rutted roads almost daily, visiting and talking about God to the people. While several hundred Masai in other parts of the South Kenya Conference have accepted Jesus, the villages near Narok are scattered and the people more nomadic, often building their villages far from the road. Daniel did what he could but was unable to reach as many Masai as he wanted. He prayed for guidance as he attempted to reach these people, his people.

Daniel's three churches were miles apart, and his parishioners widely scattered. Still the Lord blessed his efforts. Leah stood by his side, happy to see him working for the Lord, and the Narok community compared the clean home and yard and life-style of this dedicated family with their own. Soon all those around came to love and respect Daniel Sinkira and his family.

Daniel and Leah's cup of happiness overflowed on April 24, 1982, when union and conference men ordained Daniel a full minister of the gospel. Soon after this, and following two years of successful ministry at Narok, the South Kenya

Conference requested that Daniel return to the Kilgoris district to work more directly with the Masai in his home area.

Daniel accepted the challenge after talking it over with Leah. Problems loomed as they made preparations for the move. Meshack and Naomi were both enrolled in school for the year, and Kenya schools make no allowances for moving. They would have to complete the school year, not yet started, before Leah and the children could join Daniel in his new pastorate.

"How will you manage with four children when I will be so far away?" Daniel asked. But Leah, with experience in being separated and having seen the Lord care for her at other times, replied, "God will take are of us. You have a work to do and must go where you have been called. We will join you as soon as school is out."

At Kilgoris Daniel began working among people he had known for years—reclaiming some, encouraging the weak, and rejoicing with the strong.

Visits to Leah were expensive and difficult. Public bus was least expensive, but not practical. Routing didn't include Narok; one only arrived there by a very round-about way. The *matatu* took less time but was uncomfortable and nerve-racking. The occupants slid from one side of the *matatu* to the other as the driver made the best possible time in reaching his destination by swerving around one sharp corner after another. But none of this discouraged Daniel Sinkira and his family, who are still dedicated to telling his people that Jesus is coming soon.

In some ways, the year seemed forever. How it pleased Daniel when Leah and the children were able to join him at the end of the school year.

Following his ordination to the gospel ministry, Daniel wrote, "To my family and me, this day was a very special day. My wife is happy that we are now set apart for the work of the Lord forever."

Surely the Lord will reward such dedication!

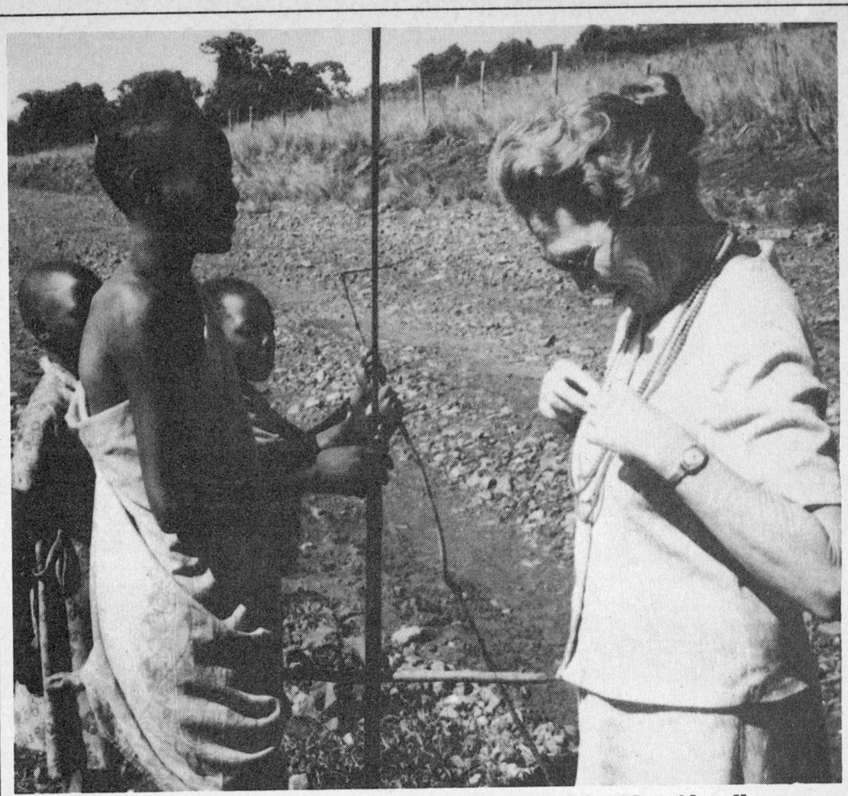

Author admiring beads placed around her neck by Masai herdboy.

Typical rest posture of a Masai herdboy.

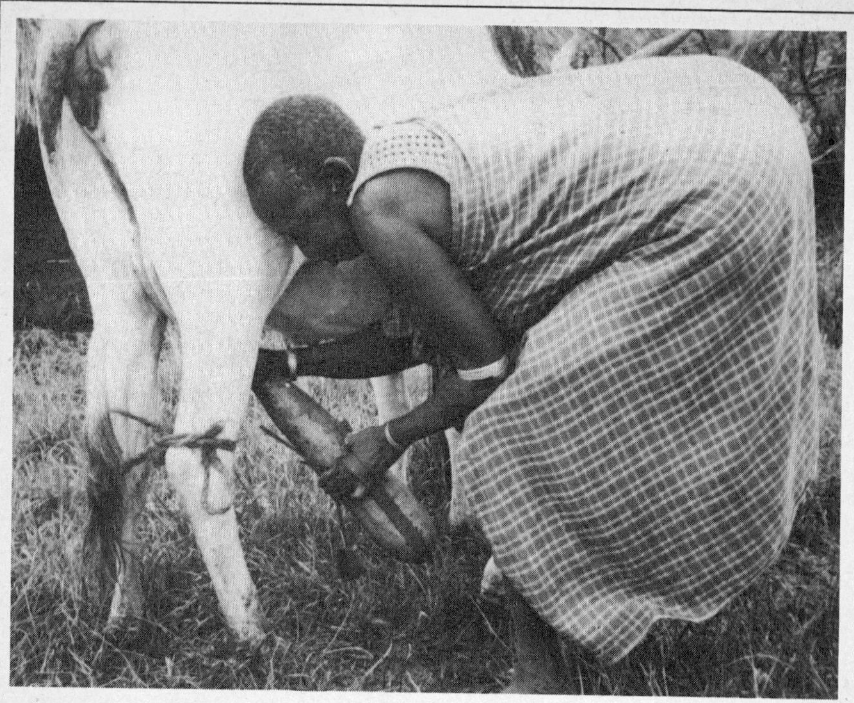

Woman milking into a gourd dusted with charcoal to keep the milk sweet.

Due to Christ's influence in his life, Sinkira became a worker for God and took the name of Daniel as his first name.

Pastor Daniel Sinkira by the Oloiborsoito Church, where he was married.

Daniel Sinkira and Leah, his wife.

Daniel and Leah in front of the church at Narok.

The Narok church interior. The membership stands at 350.

Daniel preaching at camp meeting in an outdoor area.

The Sinkira family. Daniel and Leah holding baby Jane, Naomi, Norah, and Meshack.